Hanna pulled back before she gave in to the temptation to kiss him

That blue stare bored into her and held her captive.

"I need to go."

"Don't." Before she could take a step, he pulled her to him. His lips covered hers, demanding and receiving. His tongue exploring and enticing.

Pressing her body into his embrace, she rubbed her hands up his back and tangled them around his neck. The short hair at the nape of his neck tickled her fingertips, but she could do little more than groan in satisfaction at the familiar scent of shampoo and sweat.

"Hanna," Vince whispered against her lips as he held her tight against him. "I don't want to be your friend."

Dear Reader,

Although the characters and businesses created in this book are fictitious, Marble Falls is real—a cozy little town in the beautiful Texas Hill Country. If you've never been to Texas, driving across the huge state is like traveling to several different countries. From the towering pines in east Texas to the gulf coast to the mountains in Big Bend, each area is unique. However, the Hill Country in the heart of the state is one of my favorite locales. Rolling hills, lakes and rivers color the landscape of the many small towns famous for mouthwatering home cooking, rafting, antiques and fields of wild flowers. Marble Falls is nestled beside a lake, created by damming the Colorado River. Nice friendly people, a relaxed small-town feel and beautiful scenery create a perfect backdrop for *Second Chance Dad*.

I hope you enjoy the story and your little trip to the Texas Hill Country as much as I enjoyed writing it. As with all my heroes, there is a little bit of my dad in Vince. That dry sense of humor and unique parenting style that forms a special bond between father and daughter.

Pamela

Second Chance Dad
PAMELA STONE

TORONTO NEW YORK LONDON
AMSTERDAM PARIS SYDNEY HAMBURG
STOCKHOLM ATHENS TOKYO MILAN MADRID
PRAGUE WARSAW BUDAPEST AUCKLAND

Recycling programs
for this product may
not exist in your area.

ISBN-13: 978-0-373-75351-2

SECOND CHANCE DAD

Copyright © 2011 by Pamela Stone

This edition published by arrangement with Harlequin Books S.A.

For questions and comments about the quality of this book please contact us at Customer_eCare@Harlequin.ca

® and TM are trademarks of the publisher. Trademarks indicated with ® are registered in the United States Patent and Trademark Office, the Canadian Trade Marks Office and in other countries.

www.eHarlequin.com

Printed in U.S.A.

ABOUT THE AUTHOR

Ask how an accounting graduate who spent twenty plus years in the technology field became a romance writer. Take an only child with a wild imagination coupled with summers in the country and lazy walks on one grandparent's farm or reading romance novels at the other and you have me.

Writing is pure escapism. Childhood imaginary friends developed into teenage fantasies. Later as a mother of two young sons, I began writing to keep in touch with the adult world. I continued writing as a method to wind down after exhausting days in Corporate America. Either way, writing keeps me sane. Cheaper than a therapist and tons more fun.

I still reside in Texas with my childhood sweetheart and husband of...well, we won't mention how many years. In my spare time I enjoy traveling and spending time with friends and family, especially our adorable grandkids.

Books by Pamela Stone

HARLEQUIN AMERICAN ROMANCE
1267—LAST RESORT: MARRIAGE

Don't miss any of our special offers. Write to us at the following address for information on our newest releases.

Harlequin Reader Service
U.S.: 3010 Walden Ave., P.O. Box 1325, Buffalo, NY 14269
Canadian: P.O. Box 609, Fort Erie, Ont. L2A 5X3

I'd like to again thank my editor, Johanna, for believing in my writing and helping bring this book to life. My family for their patience and support. My critique partners, Linda and Juliet, without whom this book might have never gotten written. I'd also like to thank my fans for buying my first book and giving me the confidence to put myself out there again!

Chapter One

Something was badly amiss in the Texas public school system: Hanna Rosser's straight-A son did not participate in fistfights.

Hanna pulled into the parents' parking lot of Marble Falls Elementary and tried to keep her cool as a motorcycle roared into the spot she'd been eyeing. Calmly she parked her white Volvo SUV two spaces down and tried not to notice how the tight denim hugged the guy's long legs as he slid off the macho contraption and headed up the sidewalk, unbuckling his helmet.

Trade the helmet for a Stetson and the Harley for a stallion and he'd epitomize the phrase *long, tall Texan*. Six feet and some change, dirty cowboy boots and a swagger that said he couldn't care less what anyone else thought.

Slinging the helmet by the leather strap, he jabbed his fingers through his disheveled hair and then opened the heavy glass door. He stepped back, allowing her to precede him into the hall. For each of his long strides Hanna made two, her heels tapping on the shiny waxed tile in her rush toward the office.

Ashton's first day in a public school and he'd been involved in a fistfight? This couldn't be happening.

She reached for the metal handle of the office door, and again, Mr. Tight Jeans leaned around and held it open for her.

Deep dimples bracketed his mouth. "After you, ma'am." His voice held the same interesting mix of smooth and tough as his jeans.

Leading the way into the office, she wondered if this man's bully son was the one who'd taken a swing at Ashton. Fighting hadn't been an issue in Ashton's private school back in Dallas. She'd certainly brought him up to know better than to strike another child.

The secretary stood and nodded. "Ms. Rosser. Vince."

Vince? Hanna glanced at him from the corner of her eye as he flashed those killer dimples at the little redhead behind the desk. This guy was on a first-name basis? Oh yeah, undoubtedly his son had been picking on the new sixth-grader.

"Please take a seat. We're just waiting on one more parent, and then Principal Montgomery will see you."

Vince stood until Hanna sat, and then folded his long, lanky frame into a matching wooden chair, placing his black-and-silver helmet on the one between them with a clunk. She inched farther away as Vince crossed one leg over the other, his giant cowboy boot further staking his claim on the center chair.

Please God, don't let Ashton's asthma have flared up. Was her baby boy okay? Richard would have a hemorrhage if any harm had come to his son.

A photocopier occupied one corner of the office, copying, collating and stapling, the noise adding to her nervousness and humiliation during the excruciating wait to go before the principal. The entire experience made her feel as guilty as if she'd been the one called to the office instead of her child.

"So who is the other parent?" Vince asked the secretary.

"William Baer." She shuffled papers on her desk and looked up as the door creaked and a stocky male entered the office. Even sporting a company emblem on the breast pocket, Mr. Baer's navy golf shirt and tan Dockers looked more respectable than Vince's denim ensemble.

Vince stood and shook his hand. "Hey, Will."

"Vince."

Hanna smoothed her skirt as she stood, uncomfortable with the way Mr. Baer's gaze roamed up and down her frame.

He extended his hand. "William Baer, ma'am. I don't believe I've had the pleasure."

Accepting the overly zealous handshake, she almost choked on his sweet aftershave. "Hanna Rosser. We just moved to the area this weekend."

"Well, I must say, you're a most welcome asset to Marble Falls."

Vince cleared his throat and for the first time actually seemed to notice Hanna's appearance. Without comment, he turned his attention back to the secretary. "So, what's the problem?"

She punched a button on the phone and within moments Principal Montgomery stepped out. Hanna had met the woman literally six hours earlier when she'd enrolled Ashton. Approximately forty, tiny, rather attractive in a no-nonsense sort of way. Short blond hair tucked behind her ears, black slacks and a bright-red blazer. "Please, step into my office."

Both men stood, allowing Hanna to walk between them before entering.

Principal Montgomery nodded to each as they entered. "Ms. Rosser. Mr. Baer. Mr. Keegan."

Hanna did a double-take at the girl sitting between Ashton and the other boy, as if separating the boys so they wouldn't throw more punches.

Hanna rushed to Ashton, scanning him for any injuries. She gasped and ran her finger over the caked blood at the corner of his split lip. Jerking away, Ashton scowled and glanced at the other two kids.

Taking the hint, Hanna pulled her hand back, still assessing the damage. One shirtsleeve had been half ripped from the seam, Ashton's lip was swollen and his dark hair was a mess, but he held the ice pack in his hand, not to his lip. At least, his breathing wasn't labored, and there was no wheezing.

Afraid she'd embarrass him further, Hanna resisted the urge to pick the sprigs of grass out of his dark curls.

Taking a stance behind Ashton, Hanna watched the men as they waited for the case to be presented and Principal Montgomery to deliver her verdict.

"Who wants to speak first?" the principal asked the children.

Mr. Baer turned to the pudgy boy. "Billy, did you start this?"

"No way. I was just minding my own business."

"So who hit who?" Mr. Baer demanded.

Billy shrugged and looked sheepish.

Hanna couldn't imagine that Ashton had hit him at all, much less first. "Did you strike this boy?"

Ashton mimicked Billy's sheepish shrug. "Not first."

"So who threw the first punch?" Principal Montgomery asked.

Ashton cut his eyes sideways at the girl while Billy shuffled his dirty sneakers.

Mr. Tight Jean's gaze landed on the girl with the falling-down ponytail and grungy jeans. "You're unusually quiet, Mackenzie."

The girl stood and placed her hands on her slim hips. She had a good three inches on either boy. "He asked for it."

"Nuh-uh." Billy leaned into her face. "You hit me first. I don't hit no girls, not unless they punch me first."

Ashton stood to the side while the other two faced off.

"Mackenzie, did you hit Billy?" Vince asked.

"He's a yellow-bellied scum reptile, Dad. He's always

picking on people who won't fight back just so's he feels tough."

Hanna stared at father and daughter. Both tall and slender with the same sandy-blond hair, Mackenzie's only a shade lighter than her father's. Even their honey-tanned complexions matched.

Mackenzie's left eye sported a darkening bruise, but her father didn't seem overly concerned. Hooking his thumbs in his pockets, Vince raised an eyebrow at Mackenzie. "Was Billy picking on you?" The guy's eyes were the same blue-denim color of his jeans as he matched stares with his rebellious daughter.

She didn't back down. "He knows better than to mess with me, but he figured Ashton was fair game showing up in church clothes and all." She flipped her bedraggled hair behind her shoulder and glared at Billy. "Didn't count on getting whipped by no girl when you picked on my friend, though, did ya?"

With a bruise on his chin, the remains of dried blood in his nose, on his upper lip and down the front of his dirty white T-shirt, Billy had obviously taken the worst of the beating. But he too held his ice pack in his hand instead of to his bruised face.

"Billy?" his father asked, but Hanna couldn't decide whether his perplexed expression had more to do with his boy hitting a girl or being bested by one.

"It weren't no fair fight. Two against one. They ganged up on me."

Glancing at Ashton, Hanna was stunned that her son's bruised lip actually snarled as he took his spot beside Mackenzie, toe to toe with Billy. "Don't mess with me if you don't want to fight."

"Ashton!" What had happened to her mild-mannered son? "Sit down."

William turned to Vince. "So what are we going to do about this?"

Vince slanted a grin and jabbed his fingers through his sandy hair, only tousling it more than it already was from the helmet. "Maybe you should warn your boy not to tangle with my daughter."

Was he insane? Holding her breath, Hanna waited for the other shoe to drop. Her friend's son in Dallas had once had charges filed against him for hitting another boy on the soccer field, and they'd ended up in court. The boy had received forty hours' community service. Just the kind of ammunition her ex could use in court to make his case that Ashton would be better off in Dallas with him and his new girlfriend.

Instead of the anger she'd expected, William Baer simply rubbed his forehead and grinned.

Both men were morons to make a joke out of this.

The principal motioned for the kids to sit as she remained behind her desk. "Totally unacceptable behavior. Billy and Mackenzie, you two are in this office way too frequently. Ashton, as you're new here, I'm going to withhold judgment. But you're starting out on shaky ground. You're all assigned to ISS for the remainder of the week. Tomorrow morning you will report to the office, collect your assignments and proceed to the library. In addition, I expect a five-page report from each of you by Friday on how you're going to learn that violence doesn't solve problems and how to get along. There will be no more incidents. Understood?"

"Yes, ma'am," Ashton said, but he flashed Mackenzie a conspiratorial grin.

Billy shuffled his feet. "I promise."

Mackenzie returned Ashton's grin. "Okay. As long as you make Bully Baer sit at a different table."

THE EARLY-SPRING WIND popped the flag and clanged the cable against the flagpole in front of the school as Hanna shuffled

Ashton toward the SUV. She couldn't believe he'd actually gotten into trouble, much less a fistfight. At least nobody had mentioned involving the police. She folded the form she'd received explaining In School Suspension and the possible consequences if this did not resolve the behavior issue.

Now that the divorce was finalized, she was fighting to regain control of her own life. She hadn't expected her control of Ashton to be tested so quickly.

Vince and Mackenzie stood on the sidewalk beside the macho motorcycle, both holding helmets. Was he actually going to drive his daughter home on that unsafe vehicle?

Ashton waved goodbye to Mackenzie, but Hanna pointedly ignored Vince Keegan. With any luck, Ashton's friendship with Mackenzie would run its course quickly. Hanna had hoped he'd pick his friends more wisely.

He carefully placed his backpack in the backseat and buckled his seat belt. "Sorry, Mom."

Staring in the rearview mirror at those deep-brown eyes, she wanted to reach back and ruffle his curls the way she did when he was little. "I'm sorry you had such a horrible first day."

"It wasn't that bad, just some of the boys kept messing with me. Walking by my desk and knocking my pencil off. No real biggy. Morning recess was okay. I was talking to Ms. Jones. But at lunch, I didn't have anybody to sit with so I found a seat at one end of a table when Billy and these other guys crowded me. Billy knocked my milk over into my plate. He said he was sorry, but his grin was all full of meanness and the other boys laughed like it was a big joke."

"I'm so sorry, sweetie." Hanna stopped at a four-way intersection and looked back at Ashton.

He shrugged. "That wasn't so bad, either. But then at afternoon recess Billy kept calling me names, and Ms. Jones wasn't noticing since she was talking to another teacher."

Visibly brightening, Ashton continued. "So I'm standing there wondering what to do, and Mackenzie swoops in like Wonder Woman. She shoves Billy and tells him to back off. He shoves back, and I don't know who hit who, but I couldn't just stand there like a wuss and let a girl fight my battle, you know? So Billy grabbed Mackenzie's ponytail, and I socked him in the nose." Ashton's eyes sparkled with pure male elation. "Blood spurted out like a fountain, just like in the movies. It was cool. He swung back and busted my lip against my tooth, but it didn't hurt much."

"Ashton, I do understand. But this behavior cannot continue. You should resolve your problems with your words and not with your fists. No exceptions. No excuses. Okay?" She didn't mention that his lawyer father would twist such incidents to seal his argument that Ashton belonged in Dallas. "Your asthma didn't flare?"

"No, Mom. Anyway, I had my inhaler."

As they pulled away from the intersection, Ashton pointed to the Super Wal-Mart. "I need some new clothes before tomorrow."

Snapping her gaping mouth shut, Hanna wondered who this boy was and what he had done with her son. "You want to buy clothes at Wal-Mart?" She hadn't been in a Wal-Mart in fifteen years. To her knowledge, Ashton had never set foot inside one.

"Yeah. Mackenzie said they have jeans. I want the kind that looks like you've been playing in them already. And she said you can buy three-packs of T-shirts."

Oh—my—God. "We can get you some jeans and shirts at the mall this weekend."

"No!" He looked frightened, almost horrified at the thought of waiting four more days. "I have to have Wal-Mart clothes tomorrow or Bully Baer will smear me all over the playground."

Wal-Mart. She cringed at Ashton's ruined polo shirt. She hadn't thought twice about paying fifty dollars for that shirt at the Galleria last summer. Only three days living back in Marble Falls and she was already considering updating her son's designer wardrobe at Wal-Mart? Would Bluebonnet Books ever generate enough profit that she could again afford to buy her son designer clothes?

Chapter Two

Punching Billy Baer! Vince followed Kenzie's little red electric bicycle into the garage and parked the Harley next to it. They both slid off and placed their helmets on the respective seats. It amused him that she mimicked everything he did. He tugged on her ponytail as she adjusted her backpack. She wrapped her arm around his waist, he wrapped his around her shoulders, and they headed across the backyard playing their game of trying to see who could put their foot in front of the other one as they walked.

He watched her small sneaker jab in front of his boot in the tall grass and figured he'd better mow tonight or old Mrs. Haythorn would be over here cutting the lawn for him.

Boo stretched his paws out in front of him and yawned from his afternoon nap, his rear end straight up in the air and tail wagging in excitement as they climbed the three stone steps onto the back porch. Kenzie turned Vince loose and squatted, throwing her arms around the gigantic red beast. "Hey there, Boo. You should've been at school today. Bully Baer was a total dweeb again."

She giggled as Boo's long pink tongue lolled out and licked her neck in unconditional adoration.

Vince headed into the kitchen, closely followed by Kenzie with Boo trotting along behind. The screen door slammed shut behind them, and the dog sat his butt on the floor and waited patiently while she tossed her backpack on the chair and handed him a doggie biscuit out of the daisy-painted canister on the bar.

The mutt stretched out full-length on the cool vinyl and made short order of the biscuit. Kenzie grabbed two sodas from the fridge and gave one to Vince on her way to the pantry.

Vince popped the top and dodged Boo's flapping tail. If he'd realized he was allowing Kenzie to adopt a horse seven years ago, he might have been more insistent on one of the smaller pups. But she'd tossed a fit at the animal shelter for the red puppy with the huge feet. It had reminded her of her favorite TV show at the time, *Clifford*. Part Irish Setter and part Great Dane, Boo was a bottomless pit. Girl and dog were inseparable, leaving Vince to justify why half his grocery bill went for dog food.

"So, who's the new kid?"

Rummaging through the pantry, Kenzie retrieved a package of cookies and plunked it and her soda on the bar. She hoisted herself onto the bar stool and waved a cookie. "Ashton and his mom just moved here from some fancy park in Dallas. His dad lives there with his new, very hot girlfriend."

"Highland Park?"

Kenzie nodded. "Yeah, I think so."

"Highland Park is a ritzy, old-money neighborhood, not a park." Vince grinned. "But what does his absentee dad and very hot girlfriend have to do with why you got in a fight over the kid?"

She took a drink and her blue eyes lit with mischief. "I couldn't just stand by and let Billy pick on him. Then I'd have been no better than Bully Baer."

Although Vince was proud she was willing and able to stand up for herself, and evidently others as well, he wasn't sure that noble motive was entirely the root of this incident. "You used this new kid as an excuse to punch Billy Baer."

Kenzie washed her cookie down with strawberry soda. "Stupid bullies tick me off."

"Agreed. But next time you might give the new kid a chance to fight his own battle, or Billy and his gang of misfits will peg him for a sissy and continue to make his life miserable." Vince tossed his empty can in the recycling bin and grabbed the pickup's keys off the counter. "I've got to run over and check on the crew working on the Andersons' dock before they skip out early and we miss our deliverable. Want to go with?"

"Come on, Boo." She sealed the package of cookies, jammed her pink ball cap with the ridiculous logo Pink Is The New Black on her head backward and picked up the soda. "We need to stop for dog food."

"Woof," Boo chimed in, trotting out the door behind her.

Out of dog food already?

AFTER CHECKING ON the progress of the Andersons' dock, Vince pulled into the crowded Wal-Mart parking lot. He loaded a fifty-pound bag of dog food, two boxes of breakfast cereal and other odds and ends into the cart and headed across the store for new socks for Kenzie. Where they disappeared to once inside the dryer was a mystery, but he'd never done a load of laundry and had the socks come out even. There had to be a huge cosmic black hole somewhere full of all sizes and colors of mismatched socks.

Of course, they didn't make it past the video-gaming department without her spotting a game she couldn't live without. "Dad, they have Wii NASCAR. Can we get it?"

"Forty bucks? You got that much saved from your allowance?" He flipped the game over and checked the rating.

"I have eighteen. Come on. You'll play it as much as me,

you know you will. If we get it, you can deduct the other two dollars for my half from my allowance this week."

Her keen rationalization always suckered him into helping fund her plans. He tossed the game in the cart. "Fine, but don't try to hit me up for the full ten dollars when you only get eight Friday."

"Thanks, Dad." She gave him a hug and headed toward the girls' department. "I'm going to wipe you off the track when we get home."

"In your dreams." He should count himself lucky that she had only asked for one game this trip. "No games until all your homework is done. And you get me called up in front of Principal Montgomery one more time and the Wii goes in the closet until school's out. It's been years, but I distinctly remember graduating sixth grade. I've got no desire to go back."

"It's okay, you're cool. You still like to play games. And you slowing down in your old age is what gives me the edge so I can win."

Picking through the bins, she selected a plastic bag of assorted socks plus a new purple-striped sleep shirt and Vince herded her in the general direction of the checkout. His day had started at 5:00 a.m., and he still had to get home, unload the groceries, throw something together for dinner, make sure Kenzie did her homework and took her bath, and only then could he get time to work up the bid for the two docks on Lake Travis. He grinned. And now there was NASCAR to work into the schedule.

"Ashton! Hey!" Kenzie called out, making a ninety-degree turn into the boys' department.

"Hey." The kid Kenzie had defended at school today stood in the boys' jeans section grinning at her. His mom didn't look nearly as pleased.

"Can you make Mom understand that these faded jeans are way cooler than those dark-blue ones?" he asked.

Kenzie held the offensive jeans in front of her. "Geesh, these things are so stiff they can stand up even when you aren't wearing them."

Vince ventured a grin at the mom. She looked even more uptight here than she had at school. Chocolate-brown eyes and lashes, complexion like melted vanilla ice cream. He'd seen some bow-shaped mouths, but hers was classic. A pair of designer sunglasses perched on top of her dark curls. If he tugged one of those soft little ringlets, it'd probably spring right back into place.

She offered a half grin and took the jeans out of Kenzie's hand. "These are nice. Tailored."

"And Bully Baer will call me a nerd," Ashton said.

"It's not my fault if Billy Baer has no taste," Ashton's mother defended in a gravelly, Demi-Moorish voice. "I won't have you going to school in sloppy, faded clothes."

Vince leaned on his cart, staying out of the fight as he followed the woman's quick perusal of his daughter's faded jeans and pink ball cap. She dismissed Kenzie's casual style, picked through a rack of three-button golf shirts and selected a banana-yellow-and-white-striped number.

This boy was going to get the crap beat out of him tomorrow.

With a mutinous scowl, Ashton slunk into the dressing room, the jeans and golf shirt grasped in a tight fist.

Undeterred by the mom's ruling, Kenzie plowed through a shelf of faded jeans as if she could override her if she found just the right pair.

"Vince?" Hanna's sultry pronunciation of his name sounded sexy as hell. She stared at him as if she'd rather be anywhere else than standing in the boys' department at Wal-Mart. "I'm sorry, I don't believe we've actually been introduced."

"Pardon my manners." He grinned and extended his right hand, hoping to at least get along, seeing as how their kids seemed to have hit it off. "Keegan. Vince Keegan. Nice to meet you."

"Hanna Rosser." There was a definite wariness as she brushed his hand with those long, delicate fingers.

He gave her right hand a gentle squeeze, avoiding the huge emerald solitaire. "Kenzie tells me you and Ashton just moved to town."

"Last week. And it's *back* to town. I grew up here."

She didn't sound too happy about that. "Right. And you and your mom are opening a bookstore in the old souvenir shop just off 281."

"How come I'm not surprised you know that?" She pulled her hand away, then adjusted the shoulder strap on her neat little purse. Judging from those woven *C*s on the fabric, he'd take bets it wasn't the fifty-dollar-knockoff variety. Her left hand was bare, with a conspicuous pale circle around her ring finger.

"Small-town grapevine. Can't beat it. When do you open for business?"

"Next week. Mom's been overseeing the renovation the past couple of months while I handled the ordering and—" she appeared to have lost her train of thought "—wrapped up some things in Dallas." Frowning at the video game in his cart, she didn't even look up. "We're including a large children's section. Mackenzie might find some books she'd enjoy."

Wow. He'd totally bombed as a father just because he allowed his daughter to play video games? What did Ms. Rosser have in her cart? He hooked his thumbs in his pockets and looked around, but there were no other carts in sight. How could anyone come to Wal-Mart and manage to leave without at least a dozen items? "Maybe I'll bring her by."

Ashton shuffled out, looking like a striped banana stuffed in dark jeans, his turned-down mouth showing he was almost as unhappy as he'd been earlier sitting in front of Principal Montgomery's desk. "Mom."

Kenzie handed him the faded pair she'd selected and a dull green T-shirt.

Clutching the ensemble, Ashton looked to his mother for approval. "No way, Ashton."

"Might help him fit in," Vince said, pitying the kid.

Hanna tugged at one of her short curls and the little wrinkle between her brows deepened. "I believe I know how to dress my own son."

Maybe the woman could have the kid's shirt monogrammed to match the beige initials on the collar of her starched white blouse.

Vince leaned in and whispered. "Faded jeans, fourteen ninety-nine. Green T-shirt, five bucks. Boy's self-confidence, priceless." Even the faint whiff of Hanna's perfume smelled expensive.

Her big brown eyes scorched through him, then focused on her son's face. She blew out a deep breath. "Try them on."

Clutching the faded jeans like a trophy, Ashton raced back into the dressing room.

"So anything with a decent brand is still taboo in Marble Falls?"

"There are plenty of people around here who have a taste for expensive clothes, but they aren't exactly the rage on sixth-grade playgrounds."

Ashton bounded out of the dressing room almost as quickly as he'd entered, wearing the jeans, the T-shirt and a wide grin. "They're cool."

"They'll be more comfortable once you get them broke in." Kenzie tugged the green shirttail out of his waistband.

Judging by those ever-deepening frown lines between

Hanna Rosser's eyebrows, she wasn't any more impressed with Ashton's new fashion statement than she was with Vince and Kenzie's intervention. "Do you know how hard your father works so you can wear nice clothes?"

Called that one right. Time to escape before he ticked her off even worse. Vince jerked his head toward the checkout. "We'd better get moving, Kenzie. Boo's in the truck. Later, Ashton. Ms. Rosser."

"Mr. Keegan."

Kenzie dragged him back through the grocery section for fresh strawberries and by the time they finally worked their way to the checkout, Ms. Rosser stood at the next register, a small box of caramel chocolates on top of the faded jeans and shirt, and her nose buried in one of those entertainment rags they always stocked at the checkout to siphon more money out of people's wallets.

It was fascinating how young she looked with her attention riveted on some bizarre story in a tabloid.

They'd both checked out before Hanna noticed Vince. She clutched her two plastic bags, the rolled-up tabloid sticking out the top of one.

"So, do you think Elvis weighs four hundred pounds and works behind the counter at the Memphis KFC?" he asked.

She glanced down at the bag and her cheeks turned the most adorable shade of pink. "They must have stuck it in my bag by accident."

She shifted the bags to her other hand, fished her sunglasses off the top of her head and shoved them on her nose. As she adjusted her shoulder bag, her blouse gaped apart, giving him a glimpse of sexy pink lace against creamy breast.

He gulped and looked up, catching her eye as she noted the direction of his stare. *Shit!* What did he say now? *Nice bra there, Hanna.* "Let me know if you spot Elvis."

Chapter Three

Hanna wiped her damp forehead with the back of her hand and grabbed a handful of mystery novels from the cardboard box. Smiling, she arranged them on the shelf she'd just polished. Bluebonnet Books was just what she needed to take her mind off the fiasco her life had become. Books had always been her escape. When Hanna was young, her mother had installed floor-to-ceiling bookcases in Hanna's bedroom beside the padded window seat where she'd read to her. Books about faraway places and people with exciting lives. The stories had given Hanna a yearning for life outside of small-town Texas.

"I thought you were going to put those in the front display window to draw in folks strolling down the sidewalk. That author's on the *New York Times* bestseller list."

Taking a deep breath, Hanna straightened the books on the shelf, whether they needed straightening or not. "I plan to put some up front, too, Mom. Doesn't hurt to have a few copies in both places so they're easy to find."

"I'm sure you know what's best," Mom said. "We also need a display of the latest romances on an end cap. Mrs. Haythorn reads a romance a day. Oh, and Mr. Miller always used to lend those adventure books to Daddy after he'd read them, so make sure they're at eye level. His knees are bad."

Toting the box to the front of Bluebonnet Books, Hanna

dropped it on the wood floor, which was scarred and aged from years of various businesses that had opened their doors there. Hopefully the bookstore wouldn't suffer a fate similar to the other shops. She glanced through the large plate-glass window as Darryl and Mary Wortham strolled by arm in arm, as much in love as they had been when Hanna went off to college. How could she have been gone fifteen years and returned to find everything the same? She took a breath and considered the wisdom of going into business with her mother. True, the combined funds helped. She'd never have pulled it off without her mother overseeing the renovation and being in the store to receive shipments while Hanna was still in Dallas battling Richard in divorce court. And it would be good to have two of them to switch off managing the store until they could afford to hire additional help. Plus Norma Creed needed something to keep her busy and out of everyone else's business.

But after only one week officially back in town, Hanna already doubted the wisdom of spending twenty-four hours a day, seven days a week with her passive-aggressive mother. Not that she didn't love her mom, but living under her roof again after fifteen years away put Mom smack in the middle of every aspect of Hanna's life. That wasn't good in the best of situations, and right now Hanna was still trying to recover from Richard's heart-breaking betrayal and the bitter divorce.

In a few months, she hoped the store would start turning enough of a profit that she and Ashton could find their own place.

Scooping up a couple of books, she turned as a small red motorized bicycle putted up to the curb—with her son riding behind *that girl*.

"Ashton!" Her heart leaped into her throat as she dropped the books and raced out of the shop. "What are you doing on that thing?"

He slid off from behind Mackenzie and removed the red helmet, grinning as if he'd just descended from an amusement-park roller coaster. "You don't have to pick me up anymore, Mom. I got a ride."

No way! "You are not ever to get on that thing again. You could be killed."

Mackenzie threw her leg over and stood beside Ashton, removing her own helmet. What was left of her ponytail hung in tangles. "We had on helmets."

"He did not have permission to get on a motorized bicycle. That thing is small and hard to see and dangerous."

"I know how to ride it and watch for cars and stop at lights and stuff," Mackenzie said. "I'm a good driver. I took a class and got all the questions right."

"Why are you two even out of school?" Hanna checked her watch. Oh my God. She'd been so busy stocking the shelves for next week's opening she'd forgotten to pick up her son. "Both of you hear this very clearly. I won't have Ashton riding on that thing. End of subject."

Ashton stood on the sidewalk shuffling his new white sneakers. "But, Mom."

"No *but Moms*. Do you understand?"

"Yes, ma'am."

Hanna stepped aside so Dave Barkley, carrying two plastic bags, could pass on the narrow sidewalk. Mrs. Barkley had probably given him a list of groceries to bring home from their corner grocery store. All the men in town gathered each afternoon in the old wooden chairs out front of Dave's store to shoot the breeze. Hanna returned his nod and waited until he climbed into his truck. "Mackenzie, I don't know how things work at your house, but we have rules in this family. The first rule is to ask permission before doing new things. The next time you would like Ashton to do something, he has to check with me first or he won't be allowed to run around with you.

If your parents let you risk your life, that's their business, but Ashton's safety is my responsibility. Do I need to spell this out?"

The girl set her jaw, took the extra helmet from Ashton and strapped it on the bike's back bar. "Why don't you just lock him in his room until he's, like, eighteen? It'd be about as much fun as you let him have. At least nobody'd pick on him, huh?" She jammed her helmet on her head, straddled the motorized monstrosity and sped away from the curb.

Ashton squared his shoulders and glared. "Now you've chased off the only friend I have. You treat me like a baby. You dress me like a wuss. You don't want me to have any fun, ever! And now tomorrow, when Bully Baer picks on me, Kenzie probably won't even be on my side. Why do you hate me?" He slung his backpack over his shoulder and stomped past his grandmother and into the store.

"Ashton, come back here!"

Norma Creed stood in the doorway of the shop worrying the lace collar on her prim pink blouse and staring after Mackenzie. "You're wise to restrict Ashton's association with that wild child. You have to keep him safe."

"Mom, I fully realize that." She followed her mother back into the shop. "Where did Ashton go?"

Norma looked around the vacant bookstore. "You don't think he took off out the back after her, do you?"

Wonderful! Hanna walked through the narrow store, looking each way until she reached the back door into the alley where Ashton was kicking up a cloud of dirt and gravel. "What are you doing?"

"I hate stupid glowing white shoes." He jabbed his new sneakers in the dirt. "Why couldn't you buy me blue or gray? I hate it here. I don't have any friends and it's all your fault. It's worse than Dallas," he accused, spinning around and stirring up dust like a Texas dirt devil.

His unhappiness jabbed through her heart like a rusty knife. "Honey, I want you to have friends, but I have to make sure you don't get hurt and that bike is dangerous."

"I don't care. It'd be better to get hurt than to get made fun of," he said, looking away.

"Slow down before you start wheezing." She reached out and touched his shoulder, but he spun farther away. Sandy stains ran down his cheeks where the dust had turned his tears to mud. "Ashton, I love you. I just…"

He turned and raced down the alley. "I'm going home."

Norma stood silently in the door, wearing her motherly wisdom like a halo, and once again, Hanna felt like the child who had performed below expectations. "Mom, can you lock up?"

Her mother touched Hanna's shoulder. "Why don't you lock up and let me go after him? He'll calm down walking the few blocks. Take time to calm yourself before confronting him again."

Hanna resented her mother stepping in and playing the good cop when Ashton was angry at Hanna, but it probably wasn't a bad idea. "Okay, but I won't be long."

Collecting her purse from the office, Norma marched across the street to her blue Chevy, which was nestled against the curb between two tall pickups. The only time there was any real traffic was on spring weekends, when tourists descended on Hill Country to see the wildflowers.

Turning out lights and locking the back door, Hanna stopped short at the sight of Vince Keegan standing inside the shop. "Do you need something?"

For once, he didn't smile. "It's time you and I had a little chat."

"If it's all the same to you, I'm not up for any more confrontations today."

"Lady, when someone upsets my kid enough that she calls

me crying, I want to know why. And when you start telling people, especially my daughter, that I'm a bad parent, then Mackenzie's the least of your problems."

"Your daughter is out of control." The more congenial approach would have been to offer him a cup of coffee and calmly explain that his darling daughter was a bad influence on her son, but Hanna's temper won out over her manners.

His legs were slightly spread and his eyes narrowed. "Out of control? She's the most in-control kid in town."

"From what I can see, Mr. Keegan, she does whatever she wants and has no respect for authority."

"Really?" He hooked his thumbs in his front pockets.

"Need I remind you that your little hellion got Ashton into a fistfight and placed in ISS? She inserted herself in the middle of buying him clothes, completely overriding my wishes. And now she brings him home on the back of some kind of dangerous motorbike without even asking permission. This is only day two! I'm biting my nails in anticipation of what she'll do the rest of the week."

"My little hellion kept your little prep from getting his ass kicked on the playground yesterday. And best I can figure, that was her goal again with the clothes advice." Vince leaned forward and maintained eye contact, grinding his teeth. "Today she gave him a lift home because he was afraid Billy would show up before you got there to pick him up. What exactly do you take issue with?"

"Why would any sane parent buy a sixth-grader a motorcycle?"

"It's an electric bicycle, and I bought it for her twelfth birthday so she could get where she needed to be while I was working. Unlike you, I realize I can't be everywhere at once."

"Just please ask Mackenzie to stay away from Ashton. I

can't do anything about your poor judgment, but I won't put my son at risk."

His jaw ticked. "She and I took a class before she was allowed to ride it, and she only rides the side streets where any regular bicycle would go." He glanced around the store and let out a long sigh. "Why in hell am I defending myself? Since you don't seem to mind condemning my parenting style, how about we discuss yours?"

"Excuse me?" She stared at his wide shoulders. Why was it that good-looking and cocky were directly proportionate in men?

"Maybe you should reexamine your theory that keeping Ashton under your wing is the best way to protect him." His voice remained soft and mellow, but his words bit. "Maybe consider what's going to happen when something goes wrong and you aren't Johnny-on-the-spot to stand between him and danger. Might consider teaching him to take care of himself and make his own decisions."

Not hard to see where Mackenzie inherited her disrespect for authority. "So I should let him wear ratty clothes and race around town like a delinquent in training, fighting with other children?"

Vince's denim-colored eyes narrowed, but he still didn't raise his voice. "The most important thing to teach kids is judgment and how to make intelligent decisions. If you lock them in a protective bubble, when they do escape they have no idea how to function or protect themselves in the real world."

"Do not insult my son's ability to think for himself."

"He's giving it his best shot, but you're dictating how you want him to dress and act. Kids should fit in with their peers, feel like they belong. You're making Ashton a laughingstock trying to dress him like a miniature yuppie instead of a regular kid."

Blood pumped through her veins and she took a step toward him. What did this irresponsible father know about how to dress? He was wearing old jeans and a navy T-shirt, blue plaid flannel flapping in the breeze and a Keegan's Docks cap topping off his faded outfit. Clothes that fitted his self-assurance and tight body like a glove. "You justify letting Mackenzie run wild as teaching her to make wise decisions? Might I ask what her mother thinks of this approach?"

His features stiffened. "Mackenzie doesn't have a mother."

Crap. Leave it to Hanna to put her foot in her mouth. Had Mackenzie's mother deserted them? Died? "I'm sorry."

He didn't even acknowledge her apology. "I can't be with Kenzie every minute, so I teach her how to handle herself." He came closer, bringing them nose to nose and continued to speak in a deep, controlled tone. "Kid gets invited to a party. All the other kids are swimming, but one kid's parents didn't teach him to swim because they were afraid he might drown. He wants to be part of the fun. Guess which kid is most at risk?"

"If the child didn't know how to swim, a responsible parent wouldn't let him go to a swimming party to begin with."

"Yeah, that's the way to raise a well-adjusted kid. That really helps him grow up and fit in, make friends." His jaw set. "You have any further issue with Mackenzie, you take it up with me." He sauntered out of Bluebonnet Books and onto the sidewalk, the bell on the door clanging in his wake.

She vibrated with anger as she locked the front door and made her way home.

HANNA FOUND ASHTON sitting cross-legged on the living-room sofa, his nose buried in his homework while her mom rattled around in the kitchen.

Giving Ashton's shoulder a gentle squeeze, Hanna put her

purse on the credenza and left him to finish his work. "Need any help, Mom?

Norma turned from the fridge. "You can wash your hands and peel the carrots."

Hanna bit her tongue. Like she was six and needed to be told to wash her hands? "Thanks for stepping in and calming Ashton down." Hanna dug the carrot peeler out of the drawer. "What do you know about Vince and Mackenzie Keegan?"

Norma ripped apart a head of lettuce. "Mackenzie is Belinda Maguire's girl. Since Belinda was killed, her father just lets her run wild. Spoils her rotten. Even in church, which is the only time I've ever seen her in a dress, she still manages to look like a tomboy."

"Belinda Maguire? I remember her from school."

"They were living in Austin. Huge pileup on I-35. Both Belinda and their older child were killed, but if I remember right, Mackenzie wasn't in the car. She was a toddler."

Putting her hand over her mouth, Hanna tried to imagine what Vince had gone through. Such a tragic loss. And then to be faced with the awesome responsibility of raising a small daughter alone. She'd think after losing a wife and child Vince would be even more protective than Hanna.

After getting the carrots on to cook, she took a break and joined Ashton in the living room. "I'm sorry if I overreacted this afternoon, but you frightened me."

He stuck the paper between the pages of the book and closed it. "You embarrassed me in front of my friend. It's bad enough that all the other kids think I'm a sissy, but now Kenzie knows I am."

"I'm afraid Mackenzie is going to get you hurt." The loneliness in his eyes made her weep inside. "Ashton, I'll try to do better if you'll exercise more caution."

He shrugged. "It doesn't matter anymore."

HANNA HESITATED IN FRONT of the Keegans' porch and looked down the street of manicured lawns and homey little houses that could have come straight out of an episode of *The Andy Griffith Show*. She allowed the fading pink-and-purple brushstrokes of the Marble Falls sunset to calm her nerves. Hanna the mother wanted to turn around and leave. What if this girl pulled another dangerous stunt and Ashton got caught in the crossfire? But whether she approved of Mackenzie Keegan or not, she was the only ally Ashton had in his new environment, and that was worth something. Hanna the still-insecure child knew firsthand what it felt like not to have a friend.

She clapped the brass knocker and waited. On the second rap, the porch light flashed on and the door swung open. But instead of a twelve-year-old girl, she faced a navy blue T-shirt stretched to the max attempting to cover a muscled six-pack. No denim jacket or loose flannel shirt for camouflage tonight.

Vince cocked his head. "Ms. Rosser."

"Please call me Hanna." She focused on his face. "I come in peace."

"Then you might want to come in off the porch." Standing back, Vince motioned for her to enter.

She stepped inside the room and whirled around as a massive reddish dog came up from behind and nuzzled her hand. She jerked her hand away and jumped sideways into a solid chest.

Vince's arm encircled her waist and he grabbed the dog's collar with the other hand. She fought to breathe as Vince leaned around and captured her gaze. "He's harmless."

The dog, maybe. Heart pounding, she stared into Vince's intense blue eyes and something inside her flipped. Hormones surging into high gear, she eased away from him. She wasn't sure whether to be more fearful of man or beast.

Vince retained his grasp on the dog's collar. "Come on, Boo. Let the lady settle in before you slobber all over her."

"I…uh." Eyeing the dog, she stood in the center of the living room and prayed for her voice to return. She didn't even trust dogs behind fences, and this one was too close and too big. "I came to apologize to Mackenzie for jumping on her today."

Vince turned the dog loose. "Lie down, Boo."

Obediently, the dog walked a couple of feet away and stretched out in front of the rustic stone fireplace. But his ears remained perked, and his black eyes focused on Hanna as if waiting for Vince to leave the room so he could pounce.

"Kenzie is at my in-laws' house for dinner."

"Oh." She was alone with Vince Keegan. On his turf! This had been a bad idea to begin with. "I'm sorry for not calling first. I just thought…" Trying not to look at the dog in case he might interpret that as an invitation to come closer, and avoiding Vince's gaze because, well, just because, Hanna scanned her surroundings. Framed family photos on the mantel, including a family shot of Vince with one hand resting on the shoulder of a small brown-haired boy as they posed beside a woman holding a lacy pink bundle of frills and blond curls.

Quickly looking away, Hanna focused on a soft beige leather sectional sofa. A large wooden coffee table with drawers and shelves under it, scattered with books, magazines and a crystal vase of silk daisies. A white king lay on its side in the center of a chessboard along with various other pieces and the rest off to the side. "You play chess?"

Vince narrowed his eyes. "Surprised?"

She adjusted her purse on her shoulder and clasped her hands together, not sure what to do with them. "Oh, no. I mean, my father played chess."

"Would you like to sit down? We could discuss the kids and figure out how not to be at each other's throats."

Sit? Okay. Sitting was good. She eased down on the end cushion of the sofa and placed her purse on the wood floor.

"Coffee is made or I have iced tea."

Boo stood and she held her breath. Vince could not leave her alone in this room with that animal. "No, nothing for me. I can't stay but a minute. I left Ashton doing his homework and my mom cleaning the kitchen. I have to get back soon and make sure Ashton brushes his teeth and gets his bath. His bedtime is nine o'clock." She clamped her mouth shut in an attempt to stop babbling.

Vince shoved the chessboard and vase of daisies aside and sat on the edge of the coffee table, only a foot from her face, his knee bumping hers. *Breathe, Hanna, breathe.* Deep dimples bracketed his full lips. "So my daughter isn't the only one in the family who makes you jumpy?"

The room closed in on her. The man was hogging all the oxygen. "I don't like dogs."

His dimples deepened as he rested his elbows on his knees and leaned closer. "I wasn't talking about Boo."

Instinctively she started to lean back from his nearness, but caught herself and held her ground. She gulped at his muscled forearms and large hands. "Look, Mr. Keegan..."

"Vince."

"I...we need to come to an understanding about Mackenzie and Ashton. I am glad he has a friend, but I insist on maintaining more control over what he does. I can't risk him getting hurt."

"He's going into middle school next year. If your goal is to keep him safe and out of fistfights, I'm not sure overprotecting him is going to work in your favor."

"I can see the wisdom in that. But I do not condone fighting."

"Me neither, unless the other kid throws the first punch. In which case, Kenzie will defend herself."

Hanna twisted her hands in her lap. "She should tell a teacher."

"And then the kid would pick on her the next day and the next because he'll take her as weak, looking for someone else to fight her battles." Vince's eyes narrowed. "Give Ashton a chance to fit in. To be like the other kids. He might come out with a black eye or busted lip, but that'll heal and his self-esteem will be stronger for having not backed down."

The intense raw masculine aura that surrounded Vince Keegan consumed her. She pictured Ashton earlier, sitting in the living room, so alone and desperate for a friend. He could benefit from some of this man's confidence. But too much physical activity caused his asthma to flare up. Richard might lack the down-to-earth, take-care-of-himself attitude Vince had, but he made up for it in polished courtroom expertise. If he learned about yesterday's fight, he'd have one more reason to yank Ashton out of school and re-enroll him in the private school in Dallas.

Hoping to keep Vince from noticing her shaking hands, Hanna stuck them beneath her thighs, sandwiching them between the cushions. "How about this? I'll loosen up on Ashton if you'll meet me halfway and make Mackenzie understand that Ashton has to ask permission before trying new things."

"Okay, and about the bike." Vince took a deep breath. "I realize you don't want me or anyone telling you how to raise your son. But Kenzie said Billy Baer and his group of misfits always wait for Ashton after school and torment him. Riding home with Kenzie saves him from getting into a fight."

Hanna closed her eyes. "Why wouldn't he tell me something like that?"

"Because he's trying his damnedest not to be a sissy! Not to run to his mommy to solve all his problems."

"Maybe I'll ask Mom to pick him up on days I can't."

"Oh yeah, his nana picking him up in a blue Chevy sedan every day is going to make him not look like a sissy. There's just a couple of blocks between Bluebonnet Books and the school. Give him some space to handle this himself."

"I want him to fit in, have friends. I guess as long as they're only on neighborhood streets and come straight home. I certainly don't want Billy Baer tormenting him."

"Fair enough." He grinned. "Now that we've resolved that, do you want to talk about what it is about me that makes you so skittish?"

Chapter Four

Hanna broke down a box and tossed it onto the growing stack, turning as the bell over the door clanged. A lady in jeans and a loose white blouse entered the shop, closely followed by an uncharacteristically docile Mackenzie.

The woman ran her hand through her short salt-and-pepper hair, actually more salt-and-cinnamon, and adjusted her enormous hobo-style purse on her arm. She was probably one of those perpetually prepared women who could produce anything from that monster purse from a wet wipe to a Swiss Army knife.

Eyeing Hanna, she extended her hand. "You must be Hanna Rosser."

Hanna smiled and shook her hand. Tiny brown freckles dotted every exposed inch of the woman.

"I'm Claire Maguire, Kenzie's grandmother." She turned to Mackenzie. "Don't you have something to say to Ms. Rosser?"

One corner of Mackenzie's mouth turned up, but the other maintained her scowl. "I won't make Ashton do anything without asking your permission first."

Claire cleared her throat and arched an eyebrow.

Mackenzie yanked off her pink cap and twisted it. "I'm sorry."

The apology was obviously coerced, but it was a start.

Hanna extended her hand. "Apology accepted. And I apologize for getting so angry yesterday. Can we start fresh?"

Again Mackenzie shrugged. "Okay."

Claire patted Mackenzie's shoulder. "That wasn't so hard, was it?"

"I guess not." She looked around the store. "Is Ash here?"

Ash? Nobody had ever called her son that. "He's at home with his nana doing his homework."

"While it's still light out?"

Hanna raised an eyebrow.

"I mean, why waste time indoors when everyone else is playing? I do my homework after dinner." Mackenzie looked at her grandmother. "I mean, that way Daddy is home to help." She grinned as if proud of her conjured-up excuse. "Can I wait outside now?"

Claire nodded, and Mackenzie dashed for the door, adjusting her pink cap back into place.

"Vince seldom has to help Mackenzie with her homework," Claire said with a grin. "He dotes on her, but she's a smart girl."

"I'm sure she is, a tad precocious maybe, but I can see the intelligence."

"Sharp like her daddy and book-smart like her mom. She whizzes through school with very little effort and maintains As and Bs." Claire picked up a copy of *Charlotte's Web* and thumbed through it. "Vince is a good son. I'm not sure how I'd have survived without him and Kenzie in our lives."

Son? Vince was her son-in-law. The woman's daughter had been gone nine years. Hanna wasn't sure what to say. "I was sorry to hear about Belinda."

"Thank you. Do you remember her?"

"We were only a year apart in high school. She was a sweet girl."

"Her family was the world to her." Claire swiped her hand across her freckled cheek. "I'd better get Kenzie home. Vince insisted she come by and apologize."

Really? "I want Mackenzie and Ashton to be friends. It's just that Vince and I have very different parenting styles."

"Vince is an excellent father."

Being his daughter's best buddy didn't qualify him as an excellent dad, but Hanna did envy the close relationship he had with Mackenzie. Richard had always been too busy earning a living to have time to bond with Ashton.

"I'm sure he is, but—" Hanna caught herself. "We just have different approaches."

POSSIBLY BECAUSE THE KIDS were in ISS, the rest of the week progressed without serious incident. Each afternoon when Hanna picked Ashton up at school, he had some story about Mackenzie's escapades, escapades that typically involved him.

Friday afternoon was no different, except they had to drive two hours to Waco to meet Richard so Ashton could spend the weekend with his father.

Ashton tossed his backpack on the floorboard and buckled his seat belt. "You should have been at school today, Mom. The teacher left the library to go to the restroom and Billy started being a jerk, called me a nerd, and then Kenzie called him a scum reptile. I thought they were going to get into it, but Kenzie didn't want to get expelled so she ripped a sheet of notebook paper out of her binder, wadded it up and threw it at him instead. World War *Three* broke out and we were winning, but then she saw Ms. James coming."

Geez. "Ashton."

He laughed. "Dumb Bully Baer was so busy pummeling us with paper wads that he didn't notice we'd stopped. So it looked like it'd snowed around our table when Ms. James came in, and paper was just flying one way so Bully Baer got in trouble, not us. And the best part was that he was really ticked that he'd wadded up his report and threw it, too, so when he was picking up the paper he had to unwad each one to find his report, then he had to copy it over."

The tendons in Hanna's neck threatened to snap. "Not getting caught is not the same as not misbehaving. You two were just as guilty."

Ashton huffed and glared at her. "Mom, you are so lame. You're never fun."

"There are many ways to have fun without misbehaving." Well, okay, that did sound lame. "Have you made any other new friends besides Mackenzie?"

Ashton let out a deep, exasperated breath. "Bully Baer, does he count? Why do you hate Kenzie? She's cool."

Mischievous and undisciplined was now cool? Following basic classroom rules and good behavior was lame? She'd hoped Ashton would avoid buying into the whole rebellious game. And he had, until he'd moved to Marble Falls. "I just think that next week when you're out of ISS, you might meet some other nice kids to hang around with. It's good to have more than one friend."

"Kenzie is the only one I have since you made me move to dumb Marble Falls." Ashton flipped down the DVD screen and snapped his headphones on. "Let me know when we get there."

Great. The first weekend Ashton was spending with Richard in Dallas and the boy was going to leave angry at her. Just peachy. Wonderful start to an already stressful weekend.

Hanna drove in silence while Ashton sat in the backseat, headphones isolating him from further conversation. He laughed at the movie, but didn't even acknowledge her. Waco was approximately halfway between Marble Falls and Dallas and where she'd arranged to meet Richard. This was the first time Ashton would be so far away from her since the divorce. What if he had an asthma attack? Would Richard know what to do? She wouldn't relax until she had Ashton back with her.

Richard's silver Lexus sat in the McDonald's parking lot, but he wasn't alone. That college student who had broken up Hanna's marriage sat in the passenger seat, her hair twisted and stuck to the back of her head with one of those huge finger clips, blond sprigs sprouting out at odd angles. She stared straight ahead and avoided looking at Hanna. Good! The little home wrecker *should* feel guilty.

Hanna gulped as Richard opened his door and came around to collect Ashton's suitcase. As always, Richard was dressed to the height of style. Gray slacks she'd bought him last Christmas and a white button-down. Both starched and pressed, courtesy of the Highland Park Cleaners. Short brown hair freshly trimmed every third Tuesday at five-thirty. Every detail attended to.

This whole situation was surreal. What had happened to their family? How had they gotten to this point? She glanced at the little blonde in the front seat. Hanna's stomach threatened her with nausea. Suddenly this girl had Hanna's family and Hanna was the outsider.

At least Hanna had primary custody. For now. She could take Ashton anywhere in Texas as long as she contributed half the expense of his transportation for designated visits with his dad.

But what if Richard didn't bring Ashton back Sunday afternoon as agreed upon? When she'd announced her intention to move home to Marble Falls to be close to her mother, Richard had insisted that Ashton would be better off remaining in Dallas with him. He'd argued that the divorce had been hard enough on their son and it would only make it harder if they uprooted him from the home and school he was accustomed to.

What if Ashton decided he missed Dallas and didn't want to come back to Marble Falls? Especially given that Hanna didn't seem to be at the top of his favorite-person list at the moment. In a couple of weeks, Ashton would be twelve and the judge would probably go along with his wishes.

Engulfing Ashton's slender shoulders in a tight hug, she breathed in his playground scent and forced back her tears. "You have fun with Daddy, and I'll see you Sunday. Do you have your inhaler?"

Rolling his eyes, he dug the tube out of his pocket and held it up as proof. "I have it, Mom."

She managed a cheery smile and prayed it reached her voice. "I love you."

"See you in two days." Ashton gave her a quick squeeze then crawled into the backseat of the Lexus and switched on his Game Boy. Was he trying not to cry, too, or was he just angry? Was this what they had to look forward to every other week for the next six years? A hundred and fifty more weekends!

Richard closed the car door and turned to Hanna. "Don't look like I'm torturing you. You just can't let him go without making him feel guilty for leaving you, can you?"

Her jaw dropped, but Richard only smirked. "You aren't totally innocent in all this, you know."

Snapping her mouth closed, she glared at him. "You're blaming me? I honored my vows, fulfilled my duties, took care of the home and family, remember?" She took a deep breath. "Ashton has an extra inhaler in his bag and the doctor's info is on a card in the side pocket just in case."

"I'm still his father, Hanna. He'll be fine."

She crawled back into her car and slammed the door before he could notice her shaking. Maybe their marriage hadn't been the most passionate, but she wasn't the one who'd strayed, and she'd be damned if she'd take the blame.

The Lexus purred to life, and Hanna waited to start her own car until Richard had pulled out of the lot and out of sight. She stared up at the giant yellow M and blinked back tears. Families and small kids inside the window gorged on chicken nuggets slathered in ketchup while others climbed in and out of the colorful playground tubes. Okay, so Ashton was too old to enjoy crawling through tubes, but he still liked McDonald's burgers.

At the thought of food, her stomach growled and she swiped the tears out of her eyes, took her sunglasses off the top of her head and put them on. Nostalgia wasn't going to buy her anything tonight. She started the car and pulled into the drive-through lane behind a dirty white pickup with ladders sticking out of the bed. A person had to eat and who wouldn't feel better after a bag of hot, salty fries?

On the drive home, she tried to think about anything rather than the fact that for every mile she drove one direction, Richard was driving one in the other and Ashton was two miles farther from her.

This was insane! Ashton was almost twelve years old and he'd been away from her before. Summer band camp. Weeks with his grandparents. But never a weekend with that other woman while Hanna was over two hundred miles away. It made Hanna's blood boil to think about that home-wrecking co-ed taking care of her child. It wasn't insulting enough that she'd stolen Hanna's husband, now she had her son. And the three of them would spend the weekend in Hanna's house! The Highland Park house she'd loved and spent years and a fortune remodeling and decorating.

Bluebonnet Books. Grand opening Monday. Think about all the things that had to be done this weekend. She needed this time to take care of all the final details. Ashton would be fine. It wasn't as if he was a baby. He was perfectly capable of making himself a sandwich even if the woman was helpless. And he'd be comfortable in his old room.

Books. Coffee. Pastries. Her life was certainly in a big mess, maybe the bookstore could be successful enough to take her mind off the fiasco Richard had made of all their lives. Other than an occasional call from her friend Tiffany, there was nothing left of her life in Highland Park.

SLEEP AT LEAST WAS SOUND once Hanna got home. She woke up early Saturday morning ready to plow into all the last-minute details at Bluebonnet Books. If she kept busy, maybe she wouldn't think about that girl in *her* house with *her* husband and son.

She left a note for her mother, who was still snoring like the little engine that could in the next bedroom, and walked to the bookstore. A late-April chill filled the air as the sun crept over the trees, turning the sky to pink and orange. Today Hanna was relieved her mother wasn't an early riser. She relished the sanity time.

By nine-thirty, when her mother strolled through the front door, cell phone to her ear, the rich aroma of coffee filled Bluebonnet Books. Hanna had arranged copies of the latest magazines on the front rack. She quickly replaced the entertainment magazine she'd been thumbing through.

Norma Creed's eagle eyes glanced at that exact spot in the display. She put her hand over the phone. "I can't believe you're planning to sell those gossip rags in our wonderful community bookstore. They're nothing but trash."

Hanna fought to keep a straight face, at least until her mother talked her way to the back office to stow her purse. Norma was the ringleader of the town gossip grapevine. The woman knew everyone's little secrets and, although she professed to hate gossips, delighted in sharing whatever she knew with anybody she ran across. That was just one of the reasons Hanna had taken the first road out of Marble Falls as soon as her high-school diploma was in her hand. Thanks to good grades and a college fund, she'd headed for SMU and a degree in English and never looked back.

So much for her great escape.

Her mother's cell phone rang again as she reentered the room. Hanna listened to a five-minute ramble about some poor woman whose husband was evidently having trouble making babies. It seemed that the only change in the grapevine in the fifteen years Hanna had been absent was that it had become turbo-charged thanks to cell phones.

Norma hung up, poured herself a cup of coffee and selected a Danish from the small box Hanna had picked up on the way in. "So, have you heard from Ashton this morning?"

Thanks, Mom. I really needed to be reminded. "Ashton is fine. He has my cell number if he needs anything."

"I was just concerned, as I know you are. How was Richard? Did you two talk?"

"Richard had his new girlfriend with him. I wasn't in the mood to stand around a parking lot and chat." Hanna picked up the empty boxes and toted them to the back. It was going to be a long day.

About the time Norma settled into organizing the tourism and travel section and Hanna thought she might get a moment of peace, who should pull up to the curb on her red bike and slink into the store but Mackenzie Keegan. Helmet in hand, she spotted Hanna. "I was just wondering if Ash is around."

Hanna stood and stretched. "Good morning, Mackenzie. Ashton is spending the weekend with his father. He won't be home until late tomorrow evening."

Shrugging, Mackenzie selected a comic book off the shelf and studied the front cover. "I knew that. But I thought maybe he'd come home early." Mackenzie placed the comic book precisely where she'd picked it up, even straightening the arrangement. "Yeah, well, he wasn't too thrilled with going so I just figured he might've gotten out of it."

Sudden warmth bubbled up inside Hanna. "Dallas is four hours away. Unless something unforeseen happens, he'll spend the entire weekend. But just for the record, I wasn't too happy he left either. I miss him."

Mackenzie jabbed the helmet on her head and buckled the strap. "I figured. So, just tell him to call my cell if he gets back early."

Hanna's day brightened. Not that she wanted to deprive Ashton of time with his father, but it was certainly a boost to know he hadn't been eager to go. She poured another cup of coffee and hummed as she arranged the children's section to accommodate the little wooden table and benches that had arrived.

She opened an adorable book of bedtime stories and "Twinkle, Twinkle, Little Star" chimed from one of those tiny embedded music boxes. Putting thoughts of Ashton out of her mind, she snapped the book shut just as the bell on the front door clanged again. She hoped they'd have this many patrons next week when the store actually opened.

"May I help you?" she asked, standing up from behind the low bookshelf and coming nose to shoulder with Vince Keegan's Henley T-shirt.

His blue eyes twinkled as he noted the tiny children's book in her hand. "Kenzie said she stopped by. I wanted to make sure she was on good behavior."

Hanna carefully placed the book back on the shelf and gave her heart a second to stop fluttering. Why did she let his presence do that to her? "She did stop by. Looked bored."

He cocked an eyebrow. "Now there's a dangerous combination. Kenzie and boredom."

"The town should be put on alert, I'm sure."

Hanna was still grinning as Norma came out of the back room, wiping her hands down the front of her navy knit slacks and leaving streaks of dust. "Did I hear someone come in?"

"Good morning, Norma." Vince twisted his cap in his hands and turned back to Hanna. "Kenzie tells me Ashton's in Dallas this weekend. I thought maybe I could persuade you to join me for lunch at the Falls Diner."

To discuss the kids? Hanna blinked. Lunch with a friend? Lunch as a—gulp—date? He didn't elaborate. Just lunch.

Remembering the scene the other night at his house when Vince's knees bumped hers still made her break out in a sweat.

Although her feminine ego was pleased by his invitation, she just wasn't ready. Her heart still felt numb toward anything that remotely resembled romance. Besides, half the town gathered at the Falls Diner every day for lunch.

What happened at the bustling little diner did *not* stay at the diner. As in any other small town, the locals gathered at the local eatery as much for the daily gossip as for the food and wonderful selection of homemade desserts.

She watched her mom frown and move to a closer shelf to rearrange the books.

Nodding toward the coffee area in the front of the shop, Hanna led him out of her mom's earshot. "With Bluebonnet Books so close to opening, I just can't spare the time."

"Fair enough." Tilting his head, he grinned, flashing those deep dimples. "Maybe another time."

She smiled. When was the last time a sexy guy had unexpectedly asked her out? A sexy guy with just a touch of mischievousness that if she wasn't careful could suck her in.

For a long moment, he just stood there then pulled a card out of his pocket and handed it to her. "I realized after you left in such a hurry the other night that we didn't exchange numbers. Just in case."

Phone numbers? She paused. Not a bad idea, given the kids and all. She grabbed a brochure for the bookstore out of the rack and scribbled her cell number on the front. "Here you go."

Vince folded the brochure and slid it into the front pocket of his jeans. "Thanks. And Kenzie mentioned a comic book she wanted."

Hanna grinned. "Let me get it."

She rang up the comic book and took the money from Vince. Their fingers brushed as he took the bag from her and tingles shot up her arm. She quickly pulled her hand back, rubbing it down her blouse. He'd been a gentleman and not stopped her from leaving the other night. But she reacted to his slightest touch and the worst thing she could do was send out sexual signals she was not ready to follow through on.

He slung the bag by the handle as he backed toward the door. "See ya."

"See ya." Hanna stared at his denim-covered ass as he left the shop. The guy did know how to fill out a pair of jeans. "Hmph. What was that all about?"

Norma walked up and followed the direction of Hanna's gaze. "Heartache in faded denim, if you're asking me."

Chapter Five

Monday afternoon, as Vince was unloading tools from the truck, Kenzie's bike pulled into the drive. Ashton jumped off from behind her and removed his helmet. "I hate Bully Baer!"

"Your mother is going to hate me if you didn't tell her where you are. Does she know you're over here?" Vince asked.

Ashton shook his head.

Vince handed him his cell phone.

Kenzie took off her helmet and looped the chinstrap over the handlebars, but she was too angry to pet Boo as he ambled up. "We were playing softball at recess and Ash was the last one picked. Bully Baer had a hissy fit when he had to have Ash on his stupid team."

Rolling his eyes, Ashton fidgeted with the phone. "Yeah, like I was thrilled to be on the 'moron' team." He kneeled down and buried his fingers in the dog's silky red mane, letting him slobber all over his face.

"Dad, they just kept poking fun at him. Every time he was up to bat they made cracks like he wasn't even on their team."

"It doesn't help that my mom gave me a stupid, sissy name like Ashton."

Vince grimaced. "I grew up with Vincent so don't complain to me."

Ashton looked up. "I guess that would suck about as much as Ashton, but at least Vince is cool."

"Now, maybe. About the third fight I got into over it, I went home ready to fight my dad for naming me Vincent in the first place. He told me it was a classy name and if I acted ashamed of it, the other kids would continue to torment me. But if I acted proud of it, like it was a cooler name than theirs, then the other kids would back down."

"Did that work?" Ashton asked, scratching Boo behind the ears. The dog's tongue lolled out in complete euphoria.

"Not always, but it helped. I actually started liking it by high school."

"Yeah, but you were probably never a wuss. I suck at sports." Ashton stood and jabbed his sneaker in the dirt on the drive. "I missed that fly ball."

"The sun was in your eyes. Anybody would've missed," Kenzie said, fisting her right hand.

Boo looked from Kenzie to Ashton as if giving his support.

Ashton did not look convinced. "I suck."

Evidently softball wasn't part of the prep-school curriculum. "Have you ever even played softball before?"

Shaking his head, Ashton looked more miserable by the second. "I played soccer one season, but I sucked at that, too. Mom says it's okay. Some people just aren't athletic and that I could beat them at chess or spelling and that they probably couldn't play the saxophone."

Yeah, not exactly going to make the boy feel manly. "Kenzie, go grab our gloves and let's toss a few around."

"I gotta go," Ashton said, giving Boo a goodbye pat and holding out Vince's phone without using it.

"Nobody is born knowing how to catch a ball. You gotta learn, practice. Now's as good a time as any."

Ashton smirked, but flipped the phone open. "I guess so."

The first few balls, Ashton ducked rather than trying to catch them. Vince finally got him past that, and left Kenzie to toss him a few while he finished unloading the truck to make room for a load of lumber he needed to pick up the next day.

Ashton's catching skills improved fast. How to hold a bat and actually make contact with the ball proved to be more of a challenge. But with Kenzie's help and about twenty strikes, Ashton finally knocked the ball down the baseline. It didn't even make it to first base, but it was a hit and enough to give Ashton cause to jump around as if he'd just won the World Series.

"Do it again." Vince straightened up the garage and kept an eye on the kids as Boo watched from the sidelines. Vince did not need Ashton to get hurt and bring Hanna down on his case.

He laid his tool belt on the bench. Actually there could be worse things. Hanna was impressive when she got all self-righteous and mother hennish.

Vince grinned at the sound of wood cracking against the ball and Ashton's "Woohoo!" If these two kept this up for a while, maybe by next year Ashton would be able to hold his own on the diamond.

Billy Baer and two of his buddies pedaled up the drive and spun their bikes sideways. "Mackenzie, you're wasting your time on the nerd."

Shit! Not what Ashton needed.

"The only time I'm wasting is any time you're around." Kenzie tossed the ball to Ashton, and Vince could see the concentration and focus but nervousness won out and he missed.

Billy guffawed. "You suck worse than a girl."

"If girls suck so bad, then why do I always get picked before you?" Kenzie boasted.

Vince put his hands in his pockets and turned to Billy. "So, you any good? Maybe you could show Ashton?"

"Dad! We don't want Bully Baer here."

Vince removed his cap, stuck it on Ashton's curly hair and took the ball from Kenzie. "Come on, Billy, let's hit a few."

Laying his bike down, Billy eyed Vince suspiciously. "Sure. Why not? I can hit better with my eyes closed than the nerd can."

Vince threw a couple of balls and allowed Billy to hit them. "Good job," Vince said as the ball sailed past the makeshift second-base sycamore tree.

Billy's smug expression grew as one of the other boys retrieved the ball and tossed it back to Vince. He let Bully Baer hit one more and his two buddies clicked fists. "See, nerd. That's how it's done."

Kenzie paced with Boo dogging her heels and Ashton looked downright miserable. Vince put a slight spin on the next throw and Billy barely made contact. The ball fouled off to the right just missing the mailbox—uh, first base.

"No fair, you didn't throw it right. One more time."

Kenzie tossed the ball back to Vince.

Adding more spin, Vince curved it directly over "home plate" and Billy swung, missing the ball as it curled to the left and bounced down the drive.

"What was that?"

"A strike, you idiot," Kenzie yelled.

"Mackenzie." Vince shut her down with a raised eyebrow. He'd probably hear about that tonight, but at least she hushed.

"Throw me another one," Billy demanded.

Vince threw him another curveball. Billy missed and flung the bat on the driveway. "You're cheating."

"Just your basic curveball. Watch any pitcher worth his salt."

"I can't hit those! They're stupid."

The shorter kid who'd ridden up with him shrugged. "Even I can throw a curveball and I'm just learning to pitch."

Billy's face turned as red as his bike.

"Here, try another one," Vince offered. "A little practice and you'll get into the swing."

Ashton grinned for the first time since Billy Baer and his team of misfits had arrived. "Yeah, even you weren't born knowing everything."

Vince tossed the ball to the kid who claimed to know how to throw a curveball. "So you're a pitcher? How about you toss some balls and let the others take turns hitting? Everybody can benefit from practice."

As they took positions, Billy shoved past Ashton. "At least I can hit most of them."

"At least my belly doesn't jiggle like a bowl of Jell-O when I run," Ashton returned.

Vince narrowed an eye. Not exactly a manly chide, but Ashton was standing up for himself. For a minute, Vince wondered if he was going to have to pull them apart, but they both took note of him and let it drop.

"What's going on here?" a female voice asked from behind his shoulder.

Hanna Rosser. He recognized that husky voice without even turning around. No woman in nine years had captured his attention the way she had. Not since Belinda... "A friendly little game of baseball."

"And what are you doing?"

"Refereeing." Vince snagged the ball Ashton fouled and tossed it back to the pitcher.

"Since when does a friendly game of baseball require a ref?"

He glanced her way. "Since Bully Baer joined the competition."

Today was the day Bluebonnet Books opened, and Hanna sported a white skirt and lacy turquoise blouse. Her dark curls glistened in the sunlight.

"So, was the grand opening grand?"

She shrugged, drawing his gaze to the curves beneath her blouse. "Not as much as I'd like. We've had a steady stream, but no big rush. Thought I'd take a break and check on Ashton."

The breeze molded her skirt to her legs, and Vince nearly groaned out loud. Long legs. Tight little ass. Those few inches of added height she had over most of the women he'd dated fueled all sorts of imaginative ideas. *Okay, Keegan. Focus on the daughter you have to raise, not lusting after her friend's mom.*

Hanna flinched as the ball bounced haphazardly off the front stoop—third base—and hit Ashton in the leg.

Vince grabbed her arm as she took a step toward her son. Her skin felt as soft as it looked. "He'll let you know if he's hurt."

Slow down. Give this time to see where it goes. She'd just come off a divorce and was probably gun shy.

Standing back, she monitored Ashton's movements until he lifted the bat to his shoulder. "This game is extremely physical."

"You ain't seen nothing yet. Next week we're tackling football."

She jerked around, anger flashing in her eyes.

Vince winked. "Kidding."

Wood cracked and Ashton's ball popped high into the trees. Billy Baer raced down the street in pursuit.

"Look, Mom!"

"Way to go, Ashton."

"Run!" Kenzie jumped up and down and squealed.

Ashton flew around the makeshift bases whooping like

a hyena. Mailbox, sycamore tree, front step and back to the drive. "Safe!"

Both Ashton and Kenzie bounced up and down like kangaroos until Ashton slowed down, wheezing.

Hanna took a step toward her son, but Ashton shook his head and straightened.

After his breathing settled, she let out an audible sigh and turned back to Vince.

"Asthma?" Vince asked. That would explain a little of her overprotective streak.

"It's improved a lot from when he was small." Hanna smiled. "Thanks for this. He sounded beaten down when he called earlier."

A thank-you? From Hanna? "You're welcome. It's a kick actually to have a boy to teach things to." For a quick second, thoughts of what it'd been like to teach his own son made him pause. Funny that no matter how hard he tried, he couldn't picture Matt at fourteen. He winced at the memory. His son would remain eternally five.

Hanna turned around. "It seems you spend a lot of time teaching Mackenzie things. She's not jealous of you working with another kid?"

"Kenzie can hold her own. A little friendly competition is healthy."

Billy puffed back into the yard and tossed the ball to Kenzie. "We gotta go."

"Good," Kenzie said in her typical "dislike for Bully Baer" tone.

He gathered his posse and the three of them mounted their bikes and sped off around the corner.

"Sore loser." Kenzie led Ashton and Boo into the house as if they'd just won a championship.

"So you're okay with sports?"

"I'm okay with Ashton smiling, and that hasn't happened

much since this whole divorce debacle." Hanna raised one eyebrow. "Just as long as he doesn't overdo. He keeps an inhaler in his pocket."

"I'll keep an eye on him when he's here." Vince said as Boo ambled out the front door, displaying a dog biscuit like a trophy. The kids followed behind with sodas. "So, Dad. You think Ash could tag along this weekend if we get to tube down the Guadalupe?"

"Mom, can I? It'd be awesome."

"That is a big *if*," Vince said to Kenzie.

Shifting from one foot to the other, Hanna glanced from the kids to Vince. "It's April. Probably too cold to go tubing."

He tugged Kenzie's ponytail. "The temperature is supposed to be close to ninety, but the weather has to hold out and it still may be chilly in the water."

"We did it last year and it was a blast because it wasn't crowded. Remember?" Kenzie grinned. "We had a picnic at the bottom of the float, then swam. Ash has never been tubing."

"Maybe this summer when it's warmer," Hanna offered.

Was her concern really for the cold water, or was it entrusting Ashton into Vince's care? Vince offhandedly said, "You could come with."

Kenzie cocked her head and stared at him as if he'd suddenly sprouted pointy ears, but she and Ashton both turned to Hanna.

"Please, Mom. Tubing and swimming and a picnic. Come on."

She squeezed Ashton's shoulder and glanced nervously at Vince. "We don't want to intrude on the Keegans' trip."

"No intrusion at all." The idea of spending the day with Hanna Rosser, in wet swimsuits no less, had already kicked his imagination into overdrive. He wasn't sure it was the smartest thing to do, but damned if she wasn't the most interesting thing to come along in years.

"So...? Cool. We're going tubing!" Kenzie high-fived Ashton.

Ashton stared at his mother as if daring her to ruin the adventure.

Hanna glanced at Vince. "We're going tubing."

Chapter Six

In spite of having been coerced into tubing down the Guadalupe, Hanna awoke with unfamiliar excitement at the thought of the day ahead. And if she were honest with herself, the man who'd instigated this adventure had more than a little something to do with that.

Just a fun day on the river. It had been a rough few months for Ashton and he'd had his life turned topsy-turvy by the divorce. Today would be a good escape. A fun adventure. Nothing in Dallas could match the friendship he'd found here. He smiled more with Mackenzie than with any friend he'd ever had.

The sun was barely up when Hanna and Ashton piled their stuff into the bed of Vince's red pickup. No magnetic Keegan's Docks signs on the doors today. However, the Keegan's Docks cap Ashton had worn home from the ball game earlier in the week had become a permanent accessory. It was the first thing he donned when he got home from school and the last thing he removed before his bath.

The pink-and-orange sunrise faded into a clear blue sky while they grabbed a quick bag of fresh-baked goodies at a local bakery. The early-morning breeze cut through her thin cotton T-shirt, but the sun should warm it up before they hit the river.

Back in the truck the kids chattered nonstop, eliminating

any awkward silence. With Ashton and Mackenzie around, Vince would play the role of doting father, not tentative suitor. It should be a relaxed day for them all.

The two-hour drive passed in no time. As they cruised into Gruene, the small community was just waking up. The pickup bounced across the gravel parking area as Vince pulled around and came to a stop under a huge pecan tree. "Pile out. Let's float!"

Mackenzie knew the drill and jumped into her sidekick role, hauling their paraphernalia down to the water. Vince didn't even have to tell her what to do. Father and daughter made quite a team. Ashton took his lead from Mackenzie, although he bounced around like a jumping bean while helping. Hanna just stood to the side, clutching Ashton's blue life jacket and feeling useless.

Vince noted the life jacket and narrowed an eye. "He does know how to swim, right?"

"Of course he knows how to swim." She hadn't forgotten Vince's analogy when they'd first argued over the kids. "But he isn't a very strong swimmer."

"It's shallow and he'll be on the tube. I'll watch him."

Holding the vest to herself, she closed her eyes, weighing Ashton's safety against the need not to embarrass him. The only other person with a vest on the rafting tour was a little girl who appeared to be about three.

Reluctantly Hanna tossed the vest into the truck. "Don't let them get too far away from you."

Vince slammed the tailgate and locked down the cover. "You got it."

"How much do I owe you for the tickets?"

Walking backward toward the river, he flashed a grin. "I'll settle for a smile."

She rolled her eyes. Okay, so she'd deal with repaying him later. This was not a date, and she didn't want him to think she expected him to pay her and Ashton's way, especially when they'd horned in on the Keegans' outing.

"Pictures." Hanna pulled her camera out of her purse.

The young college-age guide took the camera from her and motioned for her to join Vince and the kids. "You don't want to be left out."

Hanna eased in behind Ashton and smiled. The guide assumed they were a family, but then why shouldn't he?

The guide handed her back the camera and covered the rules for the group of about fifteen, then they were set. Each group stayed together to some extent.

Vince zipped Hanna's camera into the waterproof bag along with Ashton's inhaler and his T-shirt. They had a fifth tube tied to Vince's with water bottles, towels and a few supplies sealed up for the trip. Vince called out, "Kids, stay together and don't drift off. It's not deep in most places, but grab the tube if you flip."

Hanna sucked in her breath and diverted her gaze, but she kept sneaking peeks at Vince's long, muscled torso. Sandy hair covered his chest, then narrowed to a thin line, running down his stomach and disappearing beneath his dark swim trunks. Not that her ex was bad on the eyes, but Vince had at least a half foot on Richard's five foot nine inches and from her vantage point, all those inches were in his chest. Okay, so maybe a couple were exhibited in those long legs. Where Richard's legs were shorter and thicker, Vince had runner's legs.

She and the kids started out with T-shirts over their swimsuits. The water was like ice cubes when Hanna waded in. River rocks poked into her bare feet as she awkwardly plopped into the tube, but as soon as her body adjusted, the water felt invigorating.

Mackenzie shed her T-shirt before they got started. Following her lead, Ashton tossed his to Mackenzie, and she piled them on the extra tube. They both jammed their caps on their heads backwards.

Hanna scrubbed her hands over the chill bumps, but kept her wet T-shirt on. It'd warm up as soon as they floated out from beneath the trees and into the center of the river.

She'd enjoyed rafting on her high school senior trip, but she'd only had to worry about herself, not her son. She'd assumed she'd be more nervous with Ashton along. Maybe it had to do with the way Vince, in his laid-back way, always gave the impression that he was in control.

A couple of groups floated past, but there was no rush to get anywhere. The day was theirs and she loved the kids' laughter. Water had soaked through her T-shirt and in spite of the sun, goose bumps speckled her arms. The other three river rats in her party looked perfectly comfortable as both kids decided to kick water on Vince. He returned the challenge, and Hanna gave up on the T-shirt. She wasn't entirely comfortable with Vince seeing her in a bathing suit, even if she had worn her conservative navy-blue one-piece. But it was insane to ruin the day by freezing.

She eased the dripping T-shirt over her head and Vince paddled over and took it from her, then tossed it on top of the others. His perusal warmed her body even more than shedding the icy cotton shirt had.

"Having fun?"

She glanced up at the tree canopy overhanging the river. "I'd forgotten how beautiful the river is."

"Yeah, we try to come once in the spring and once in the fall when school is in session. Fewer crowds."

She returned his grin. "Good plan. The one time I came was mid-July and you couldn't see the water for the tubes."

His warm chuckle engulfed her. "Kids are having fun."

The giggles validated his remark. Hanna dipped her hands in the water and let the drops trickle through her fingers.

Ashton's scream and a splash brought her straight up, almost tipping her own inner tube over. Mackenzie's head was visible between the two tubes, but if Ashton was above water, he was hidden by the tubes. She caught a glimpse of Vince and stopped herself before she bolted into the water. Vince's body was tense and his eyes glued to the scene, but he hadn't made a move toward them.

Hanna turned just as Ashton's head popped up, then both kids stood. The water barely reached their waists, but even though he'd flipped in a shallow spot in the river, Ashton could have hit his head on a rock. He shoved the hair out of his face, and she thought he was crying before she realized he was actually laughing.

"That was cool. I flipped twice."

Mackenzie bent double, guffawing. "All I could see were flying arms and legs."

"Happy to give you something to laugh at there, Kenzie." Ashton dumped the water out of his Keegan's Docks cap and tugged it over his curls.

Still laughing, both hoisted themselves back into the tubes. "You looked like an octopus."

Releasing her breath, Hanna glanced at Vince.

He winked. "Resilient little critters, kids."

"Ash, grab hold of my rope." Mackenzie paddled closer and tossed him her tow rope. "This way we don't have to work so hard to stay together."

The tension eased out of Hanna's body and she just drifted with the water. Everyone who floated past seemed happy and the kids were never out of Vince's sight. She needed this escape as much as Ashton did.

It probably took them an extra half hour to reach the park area where they were to have a picnic, but Hanna didn't care. She wrapped her towel around her waist and quickly discarded the idea of putting on her wet T-shirt.

Exhausted from the float, they wolfed down hot dogs cooked on a rusty outdoor grill provided by the tour company. They tasted better than dinner at the Mansion on Turtle Creek. Orange Cheeto dust stuck to Hanna's fingertips as her napkin blew away. Ashton caught it and tossed it in the trash can, so Hanna settled for licking the orange dust off her fingertips.

Vince laughed. "Want another hot dog?"

She popped her pinky finger out of her mouth and hoped she wasn't blushing. "No, I filled up on cheese chips."

Vince's cell phone chimed, and Hanna turned away to give him privacy.

"Vince." There was a slight pause. "Hey, Grayson. Okay, let me see if they can spare Gutierrez on the Barkley dock for the day. I'll send him your way."

Grayson? Had to be Grayson Maguire, Belinda's twin brother. Not exactly an everyday name.

Vince hung up, made another brief call and called Grayson back. "Gray, he's on his way." She could hear rambling over the phone, but Vince didn't seem too interested. "Everything else okay? Listen, I'm kind of busy. I'll talk to you Monday." He laughed. "Yeah, or see you at the folks' tomorrow. Thanks again. I owe you."

The folks? The Maguires?

"Mom, can we swim before the van leaves?" Ashton begged. "Please. I finished two hot dogs."

Tossing her paper plate into the trash can, Hanna nodded. "Sure, I'll come down there and watch."

Ashton raced after Kenzie. "Wait up. I'm right behind you."

"Last one in is a dead fish," Vince said, yanking his T-shirt off, tossing it and his cell phone on the riverbank and charging ahead of them and into the water.

Hanna sat on the cool grass and watched Vince hoist Mackenzie up on his shoulders then toss her unceremoniously into the water. He repeated the act for Ashton, who raised his arms and pointed them over his head as Vince bent and dumped him into the river. Just hearing Ashton squeal and laugh, seeing him energized, warmed Hanna's soul. She didn't remember him ever laughing so much. She snapped a few pictures as both kids piled on Vince and tried to push him under. They did finally succeed, but he took them both with him.

After fifteen minutes of frolicking, Vince dropped down on the riverbank beside Hanna. "You could have joined us."

"I'm too full."

"Yeah, cheese chips. You were just afraid I'd get the best of you."

"Right. That was it." She refused to stare at the droplets of water dripping off his hair and onto his chest. The guy did have a certain irresistible, Southern charm. "Did you and Belinda bring the kids here?"

He skimmed water off his arms and pulled on the T-shirt. "No. They weren't old enough. We did Sea World and the circus. Made a trip to South Padre Island. Belinda always enjoyed the beach."

"Richard isn't the outdoors type. We took Ashton to New York summer before last. Caught a play and a couple of museums."

"Man, I loved New York. Spent a summer studying there between my junior and senior years. Incredible energy."

"New York?" Now that was something she wouldn't have guessed. "What was your major?"

He stretched out on his back. "Engineering. Actually I was taking classes across the Hudson in Jersey. I had landed an internship with a company in Austin that designs bridges and they worked with the college and arranged the summer in New York. We studied some of the city's bridge designs."

And now he was designing boat docks and decks. "Did you finish your master's?"

"Bachelor's, but never got a chance to go beyond that. Best-laid plans."

The damp cotton stretched across his wide chest and pulled tight with each breath. And those legs poking out from the long black swim trunks were equally impressive.

"What happened?" Norma had mentioned that he and Belinda had met at the University of Texas.

Vince closed his eyes against the bright sun, or against more questions and rubbed the stubble on his chin. "Life."

Which was more interesting, the sun glistening off the water as the kids splashed or watching Vince's chest rise and fall? He bent one knee and adjusted his position, but his breathing remained even.

Ashton struggled to dunk Mackenzie, but it didn't appear there was much danger of that. If she were a regular girl, Hanna would've put a stop to it, but Mackenzie had already pushed him under before Hanna could react.

Hanna's gaze drifted from the kids back to Vince. He had promised to keep an eye on Ashton, yet he was napping? Leaning forward, she frowned, then noticed that his eyes were half-open.

"They're fine, Hanna."

Insane. How the heck did he know what she was think-ing?

The tour vans were packing up to haul everyone back to Gruene, and Hanna motioned for the kids to come to shore. "You two need to get out and dry off."

"Mom," Ashton wailed. "Just five more minutes?"

Propping up on his elbows, Vince appeared as reluctant as the kids to leave. Yet he didn't override her command. "Come on, Kenzie. Out."

To Hanna's amazement, Mackenzie didn't even put up a fuss, just hopped out of the river and snuggled into the towel her father wrapped around her dripping shoulders. Ashton looked as bemused as Hanna, but followed his friend's lead. It seemed that the trick to getting her son to mind was simply getting Kenzie to mind.

AFTER SHOWERS AT THE BATH HUT and changing into shorts, they piled their wet paraphernalia into Vince's pickup and set out to explore the historic riverside community of Gruene. The small town looked like a postcard with antique stores and restaurants lining the main street. Hanna snapped pictures of the kids with the water tower in the background and one of Vince and the kids eating ice cream in front of the old dance hall.

"Hey, kids. I want a few pictures in the bluebonnets over there."

"Geesh." Ashton groaned. "More pictures?"

"Come on, Ash. They won't stop pestering us until we cooperate."

After a few shots of the kids, Vince grabbed her camera. "Get in the shot with them."

Hanna waded into the small patch of bluebonnets behind the children and put a hand on each kid's shoulder. Ashton let him take a picture, then picked his way out of the flowers and reached for the camera. "My turn to take pictures. You get in the shot."

Hanna sucked in a breath as Vince squatted down between her and Kenzie, his knee bumping against Hanna's. Kenzie perched on his knee and Vince put his hand on Hanna's shoulder.

"Smile, Mom."

Both she and Vince had been seeing that the kids had a good time, but the sun was beginning to set and Hanna's one hot dog was no longer enough. "Anybody up for dinner?"

"Grist Mill!" Mackenzie yelled. "It's my favorite and we can eat outside."

"Grist Mill!" Ashton mimicked although he'd never been to Gruene before today and couldn't have any idea if he even liked the food.

Vince swept one arm elaborately and led them all across the street. "Grist Mill, it is."

Mackenzie didn't give anyone else a chance to answer when the hostess asked whether they wanted outside or in. "Outside, where we can see the river."

As the hostess led the way, the kids trooped along behind her. Hanna's breath caught at the feel of Vince's hand on the small of her back, ushering her toward the table. Just a gentlemanly gesture. A very intimate, masculine, gentlemanly gesture.

Hanna hadn't been to Gruene since high school and she'd never eaten in the old mill converted into an open-air restaurant. Rustic and quaint, it sprawled down the hillside toward the river with small decks and tables nestled into the trees.

Mackenzie raced over to a corner table, one of the few that actually offered a view through the trees to the river. A group of late-afternoon tubers floated by, laughing and waving.

Ashton leaned over the wooden rail and waved back. "This is sooo cool."

Hanna slid along the bench on one side, but Ashton took his seat beside Mackenzie on the other bench. Vince joined Hanna and leaned back against the rail as the waitress placed the menus in front of them.

With all the spring pollen, Ashton was beginning to wheeze. Unsure whether she'd embarrass him or not, Hanna used a hand gesture to simulate the inhaler.

Reluctantly Ashton pulled it out and took a quick breath, then shoved it back into his pocket.

Kenzie just grinned like it wasn't anything out of the ordinary. Hanna hoped that was a sign that he'd used it in front of her before when he'd needed it.

The sun set as they were finishing their meals, and the kids raced over into the trees where there were more picnic tables. Ashton stopped to rub a black-and-white cat that was more intent on bathing his paws than on the horde of restaurant patrons watching him.

Hanna turned to Vince. His skin was a shade darker from today's adventure and his hair a shade lighter. The whole effect with the sunset colors made those blue eyes twinkle. "Amazing what one day away can do."

Vince twirled the saltshaker on the table. "Yeah, getting away from the rat race is good for the soul."

"So, will you get angry if I ask you a personal question?"

He shrugged. "Shoot."

The waitress refilled their iced-tea glasses and cleared away the dishes.

"How do you do it? I'm scared to death every time Ashton is out of my sight. Part of that is because of his asthma, but also something might happen that I could have prevented. How do you stand giving Mackenzie all that freedom? How do you resist locking her up so she won't get hurt?"

He grinned. "First off, if she's doing something she shouldn't and I don't catch her, somebody else will and let me know."

Hanna shook her head and sighed. "Ahh, the notorious small-town grapevine."

Vince raised an eyebrow then he ran one hand through his hair. "After Belinda and Matt were killed, I wanted to. God, I wanted to. My parents smothered us. We were at their house every weekend and some evenings for dinner. They're workaholics and their answer was to hire a nanny to watch Kenzie while I worked sixty-hour weeks. I tried to make Austin work, for a few months."

Hanna studied his profile as he watched the kids.

"But my in-laws loved Kenzie, too, and me. They'd lost their only daughter and my three-year-old little girl had lost her mother. She and her grandparents needed one another to fill that void. I wanted to be a bigger part of my daughter's life and Corporate America didn't allow time for that. So moving to Marble Falls and starting a business made sense on a lot of levels. I figured the best way to give Kenzie a happy life and at the same time to keep her safe was to spend time with her and to teach her to think for herself. Maybe if I'd done more of that in my marriage, my wife and son would still be alive."

"I'm sorry about your loss." Hanna felt tears well up at the back of her eyes. "You love the Maguires very much."

"I do." Vince took a long drink of iced tea and forced a smile. "They're family. Good folks."

Good folks. They'd filled the void from the loss of their daughter not only with Mackenzie, but also with Vince. And it appeared to be mutual.

"Vince, just so you understand, I'm still struggling with how to be a single parent. I've worried since Ashton was a toddler and we almost lost him to a serious asthma attack, but now I'm solely responsible for his safety. Richard loves Ashton, too, but he believes he'd be better off in Dallas. I can't give him fuel for that argument. Your tactics won't work in my favor."

Ashton wove his way through the picnic tables toward them, the black-and-white cat cradled in his arms. "Look, Mom. Isn't he beautiful? Touch him, feel how soft."

Cats and asthma, not a good mix. Yet she didn't want to ruin the day for Ashton. She ran one hand down the cat's tail. It wrapped around her hand and slid through as the cat purred like a Weed Eater. "Yes, he is. Now go put him back in the trees before you start wheezing."

That earned her a glare from Mackenzie, but Ashton turned

and eased his way back into the more open area of the rambling restaurant, carrying the cat like a precious bundle.

She felt Vince's stare. "Don't tell me. He needs a pet."

"There are breeds of dogs that are supposed to be safe for asthma sufferers."

"He has allergies." Hanna set her jaw and crumpled her napkin. "I realize he's lonely and a pet might be a good idea, but we're living in my mom's house and no way am I going to add one more stress factor to the mix."

Vince leaned around and she thought for a second he might touch her, but instead he picked up his glass. "He can stop by and play with Boo anytime. Maybe that'll help."

The way he looked at her warmed her heart, even though her common sense argued that she was on the rebound. Feeling undesirable. "It would—help, that is."

His intense gaze burned into hers, but she couldn't break away. "You look relaxed. Happy. Beautiful."

So did he. But she couldn't very well say that. "I appreciate you letting us crash your father-daughter adventure. Today's been magical for Ashton. He so needed an escape. We both did. As good as my mom is to us and as much as I love her, sometimes…"

He shook the ice in his glass and drained the last drop. "I love my mom, too, but if I had to live with her one of us would kill the other within a week. Tops."

"But you're close to them."

"Yeah, they're in Austin. And they idolize Kenzie. They're taking her to Disney World over spring break. My brother owns a large animal clinic a couple of hundred miles south, so we only see him two or three times a year."

"I'm an only kid," Hanna said. "Siblings would be good. Mom just has me and Ashton to fret over."

"Brothers mostly look for any excuse to pound each other senseless those first few years. Leo is still a self-absorbed ass most of the time. Has more sympathy for animals than people, but I haven't been tempted to take a swing at him in…I don't know, a month or two."

"Leo?"

"My parents have a strange take on baby names. Leonardo and Vincent. What's up with that?" Vince kicked back and laughed. "In middle school, we got it in our heads to take them to court for cruel and unusual punishment."

Hanna smiled. "How'd that work out for you?"

"We knew a lot of lawyers, but we couldn't come up with one strong enough to go up against our mother. A good mom, but a force to be reckoned with in the courtroom."

"Your mom is an attorney?"

He nodded. "My mom is a hell of an attorney."

Mackenzie and Ashton returned, sans the cat, and sat down. Ashton slurped the last drop of his pop through the straw. "We don't have cool places to eat like this in Dallas."

"Dallas does not sound like my kinda place," Mackenzie chimed in. "No way I could wear a dumb uniform and look like every other kid, including dweebs like Bully Baer, every day. I'd wear striped sneakers or something so as to *not* be like them."

Probably very little danger that Mackenzie would not distinguish herself in any situation. If not with her trend-setting attire, with her outgoing personality.

The lights around the restaurant came on, and Ashton's eyes sparkled. "Can we come back this summer? We can do everything exactly like we did today."

"We'll see. I don't want to impose on Mom by expecting her to run the bookstore alone all the time." Hanna wasn't sure what the summer would bring, she was so busy trying to get through the now. Bookstore. Single-parenting. Living with Mom. The Keegans.

As they made their way out of the restaurant, the old dance

hall was lit and a few couples danced as the jukebox crooned George Strait. The music filtered through the screen windows and created an ambiance of a gentler, more carefree time in Hanna's life.

Vince put his hand on the small of her back. "Ever been dancing in the Gruene Dance Hall?"

Hanna fought a blush at the warmth of the gesture. "Are kids allowed inside?"

"They'll be fine as long as they're with us. Looks like a sedate sort of crowd. No band tonight."

They wandered in and took a seat watching the couples as they stomped and swayed to the Texas two-step.

Ashton grabbed Mackenzie's hand. "Come on."

Mackenzie watched him dancing the two-step a few minutes, then held up her hands and grinned at Vince, nodding toward Ashton. "Who'd a thunk it?" She started mimicking Ashton's steps. "How do I look?"

A little awkward on the steps, but she seemed to be feeling the music as they strutted.

"Lookin' good," Vince said, then took Hanna's hand and pulled her to her feet. "I don't know about you, but I'm not about to let a couple of sixth-graders show me up." He fell into step beside Ashton. "Is this right? Show me again."

Delighted, Ashton assumed the role of instructor for the other three. Hanna hadn't country-danced in years, but she'd made sure that Ashton took lessons in all styles of dance. She'd always loved to dance, to lose her inhibitions and let the music move her. Tonight, Ashton's lessons were paying off as he beamed from ear to ear, leading Mackenzie and Vince through the steps.

Surprisingly, given Vince's lankiness, he demonstrated decent rhythm as he followed Ashton's direction. Hanna wasn't so much trying to two-step as she was just feeling the music and letting her body move. She missed a step and realized she was watching Vince more than she was Ashton. Pure symmetry.

After a bit, the adults sat and contented themselves with watching the kids. Hanna relaxed into the old wooden straightback chair and turned to find Vince staring at her. He flashed those deep dimples and sauntered over to the jukebox before stopping by the bar for four sodas.

Hanna was so parched from dancing that she gulped hers down even faster than the kids did. Mackenzie and Ashton didn't sit, just finished their drinks and hit the little section of dance floor closest to Hanna and Vince that they'd been monopolizing.

When the Bellamy Brothers catchy tune "If I Said You Had a Beautiful Body, Would You Hold It Against Me?" cranked up, Vince tilted his head toward the dance floor and winked at Hanna. "This is more my speed. Whatta you say?"

Hold her body against Vince Keegan's long, tight, sexy frame? Probably not Hanna's wisest move.

Vince tugged her to her feet. "You can't come to the country's oldest dance hall and just sit. Where's the fun in that?"

"Come on, Mom. It's not hard at all," Ashton said, wiggling his little butt.

Placing her right hand on Vince's shoulder and her left around his waist, she tried to relax. When she was younger dancing had come naturally. But now? With Vince? "Song's sorta cheesy, don't you think?"

He covered her hand and held it flat against his shoulder. "I don't know. Seemed to serve the purpose." She didn't resist the pressure of his left hand secure against her waist. The melody filled her body and she allowed the rhythm to take control and flow through her. She leaned her head back to study Vince as he buried his long fingers in her hair. She leaned into the caress then nuzzled her head against his shoulder.

God, her bruised ego craved the attention of this attractive male. She needed to feel attractive, desirable to the opposite sex.

She closed her eyes and drifted around the scarred wood floor in Vince's arms. The same dance floor where thousands of others had danced for over a century. But dancing with Vince was so different from dancing with Richard. Richard knew the steps, but Vince just moved to the rhythm and… to the lyrics. Even being five foot eight, she felt small and feminine within his arms. His heart beat against hers as they moved as one.

Everything about Vince was different from Richard. His casual approach. His subtle come-on. Okay, not so subtle given his choice in music.

"Daddy, dance with me now," Mackenzie demanded. "Let's trade partners."

The spell shattered and Hanna eased out of Vince's arms. He seemed nonplussed as he took Mackenzie's hands and flashed a smile, then spun her around and through the few couples on the floor.

Oblivious to what was going on, Ashton happily grabbed Hanna's hands. "I haven't ever, ever had this much fun."

Hanna held Ashton's hand and tried to follow his steps, but her gaze followed Vince as he twirled his giggling young daughter.

By the time they walked to the truck, Ashton was yawning at every other step. He wasn't accustomed to so much physical activity and it was ten o'clock, his bedtime. Vince took Hanna's hand and steadied her as she climbed into the tall pickup. The kids buckled into the backseat and were both asleep before they even got out of town.

Vince was quiet most of the two-hour drive as they let the kids sleep, but every time Hanna dared a glance his way, he was looking back at her. Like those tentatively exchanged glances across the high-school lunchroom, only not so tentative. It was way too soon after her divorce and too early in this friendship to be thinking these thoughts. She should not be fantasizing about Vince Keegan's long, lean body against hers. And that dimple-bracketed mouth conjured up all sorts of interesting ideas.

She stared out at the stars, so much brighter out here away from artificial city lights. The air-conditioned cab, quiet and intimate, cocooned them in the night as they drove toward home. Kids sleeping peacefully in the back. Handsome guy driving. Oh yeah, way too much like a family.

Yet, pulling into town, Hanna wished it wasn't over. Her life of late was anything but romantic and peaceful. Vince swung the pickup into her mother's drive, and Hanna smiled. "Thanks again for a fantastic day. Ashton had such a wonderful time."

He leaned forward and wrapped a curl around his finger. "So did I."

Staring into his eyes, her breath caught in her throat.

He slid his hand down her cheek and behind her neck, urging her closer. Closing her eyes to keep from drowning in the depths of his deep-blue ones, she gravitated toward his warmth, waiting, wanting.

After an eternity, his lips touched hers. Warm and gentle as he deepened the caress.

The taste and pressure of his lips moving over hers spun time away. As though she were being pulled, she tilted her head for a better angle. Scooting close, she adjusted her position to feel his heat and touched her tongue to his lips. His hand increased the pressure on her waist, urging her closer as he opened his mouth to hers, exploring and spinning her senses into a hot frenzy for more, faster, hotter.

His ten-o'clock shadow scratched her palm before she slid her hand around his neck to hold him close. She squeezed her legs together and tried to squelch the building warmth. Her tongue met his, acquainting itself with his.

The kids stirred in the backseat and Ashton sat up, rubbing the sleep from his eyes. "Are we there?"

Hanna shot backwards, away from Vince's magnetic pull and toward reality. If Ashton had witnessed the kiss, he wasn't letting on. "We're home."

Chapter Seven

Hanna couldn't get last night's kiss off her mind. Even as she walked to Bluebonnet Books on Sunday, she inhaled the scent of someone grilling outside and tasted Vince's kiss, felt his sexy mouth on hers. And whether she wanted to admit it or not, it left her aching for more.

She wasn't a teenager and rebound romances were always a mistake, but that didn't cool the warmth inside her. She glanced up each time someone came through the door wondering if it might be Kenzie come to see Ashton, perhaps with her father in tow. But Vince was probably with his family today. And it was too soon after Richard's betrayal for Hanna to rush into anything.

By Thursday, she'd convinced herself that the kiss had meant a lot less to Vince. Kenzie had brought Ashton home each afternoon on her bike right on time. But no sign of her father. Which was probably for the best.

Hanna finished checking out the last of a group of tourists and glanced at the clock. Ashton should have been here fifteen minutes ago. She watched the second hand on the clock slowly tick another few minutes, but still no red electric bike.

No need to panic or assume the worst. Except she did. Were the kids hurt? Had some sicko grabbed them after school? When Hanna was growing up here, crime was practically unheard of. But nowadays, even small towns had their share of perverts.

Maybe they'd gotten into trouble again and had to stay after school. But the school would have called, wouldn't they?

Okay, deep breath. Maybe they'd gone to Mackenzie's to play the Wii or practice softball. At one time she'd have felt confident that Ashton would call, but since meeting Kenzie, he'd become rebellious. A moody pre-teen had replaced her quiet, levelheaded, straight-A student.

She didn't have Mackenzie's cell number. She did *not* want to call Vince. It was best if she extinguished whatever spark she felt before it got started. Yet she had no choice. She needed to know Ashton was safe, and calling Vince would be easier than driving over there and having to face him.

Once the store started showing a profit, she'd get Ashton a cell phone. But for now, she had to watch every penny. Reluctantly she dialed Vince's number, her worry for Ashton outweighing her need to avoid talking to Vince.

"Vince," he yelled over pounding and the loud zing of nail guns.

"It's Hanna!" she yelled in return. "Do you know where Mackenzie and Ashton are? They didn't show up here after school."

"Just a second." Heavy bootsteps on wood and the sound of the nail guns subsided. "The kids haven't shown up?"

Her heart plummeted. They obviously weren't with him. "No."

"Let me try Kenzie's cell. I'll call you right back."

Hanna continued to watch the second hand on the clock. It circled four and a half times before her cell rang. "They're out on the lake fishing. I told them to get home."

"On the lake? In a boat?" What next? "God, if it's not one thing it's ten with that girl. Mackenzie may be allowed to run amuck, but Ashton has to be where he's supposed to be when he's supposed to be there."

"Hanna, stop. They didn't ask my permission either. They should be at the bookstore in fifteen minutes or so. You need to calm down." The line went silent.

Hanna stared at the dead phone. He'd hung up on her? Her hands shook as she slid the phone back into her pocket. Ashton knew better than this. He knew the rules. But because Mackenzie didn't have rules, Ashton didn't think he had to follow his either.

VINCE NO MORE THAN got out of the truck at Bluebonnet Books than Kenzie flew out the door. "She's really, really ticked off this time."

Vince tossed his ball cap on the seat and slammed the door. "Did Ashton ask if he could go fishing?"

"I don't know. I just asked if he wanted to and he did."

"Well, you know better than to go out in that boat without telling me and you didn't, so I'm figuring Ashton didn't ask either."

Kenzie looked down. "Sorry."

"We'll take that up at home."

Luckily there were no customers in the bookstore when Vince marched Kenzie in. Ashton sat in one of the chairs in the little coffee section, looking as if he'd lost his last friend. Which, if Hanna had her way after this, might not be far off the mark.

When Hanna saw them enter, she walked up from the rear of the shop. "Mr. Keegan."

They were back to surnames? It was like Saturday hadn't happened. Like she'd never let him kiss her. "Ms. Rosser." Vince looked between the three angry faces. "Someone want to fill me in?"

"Did I not make it clear enough that Ashton was not to try new things without first asking permission?"

Vince forced his fists to unclench. "And I thought I made that clear to Kenzie. Obviously not." He pegged Kenzie with a glare.

Ashton stared at his sneakers and Kenzie tugged at her ball cap.

Hanna looked as if she was going to blow a gasket as she turned her attack from him to her son. "You're grounded, young man."

Ashton sneered. "For how long? I go to Dad's for spring break this weekend, and you can't ground me from that. It's in the court papers. Besides, Saturday is my birthday."

"Maybe next time you'll remember to ask permission."

"He's not a baby," Mackenzie interjected, yanking her pink cap off.

"Mackenzie." Vince shut her down.

She jammed her cap back on her head and stood, sullen but quiet, to the side.

Ashton jumped to his feet and kicked the chair. "I didn't ask because I knew you'd say no. You always say no. You don't know how to say yes to anything. I'm tired of you treating me like a baby! I hate everybody calling me a nerd! I hate it here! Why do you keep ruining my life?" He grabbed his backpack off the chair and slammed out the door, the bell clanging in his wake.

Kenzie grabbed her helmet and started after him, but Vince took the helmet out of her hand. "Make sure Ashton's okay, then meet me at home. I'll put your bike in the truck."

An eerie quiet engulfed the store in the absence of the kids. "Where's Norma today?"

"It's her bridge day. Then she's stopping to make a deposit at the bank, and she and a certain teller she knows will gossip for at least half an hour." She looked up at the ceiling and blinked, returning to the issue at hand. "Vince, I can't tolerate this!"

"Settle down. I very clearly told Kenzie the rules."

Clasping her hands, Hanna dropped down in the chair Ashton had vacated. "How am I supposed to keep him safe if he won't mind? I've never been a single parent. My whole life is upside-down and I'm expected just to know instinctively how to raise an adolescent boy. I don't understand guys. They're weird."

"Women are a little weird from our perspective, too, you know." Vince squatted down in front of her and attempted to capture her gaze. "Is something else going on?"

She scrubbed her hands down her face. "Ashton emailed his father pictures of the tubing trip. Richard called this morning demanding to know who you were. You and Mackenzie are in most of the pictures. As you can imagine, Ashton was excited to tell his dad about all the fun he had, and evidently your name came up. A lot. So now Richard thinks you and I are…"

Vince couldn't hide a grin. "The guy fooled around while you were married, then divorced you for a younger woman. What the hell business is it of his who I am or what you and I are to each other? Tell him to f— mind his own business."

As she shook her head, Hanna's lips curved up. "That is exactly what I told him. But he feels it's his business if another man is spending time with his son."

"Male ego." Vince figured the guy was probably having second thoughts now that he could no longer control Hanna. "It has nothing to do with Ashton and everything to do with you. It's fine that he's moved on, but he sure as hell doesn't want another man to have you."

"That at least gives me some pleasure." She wiped her eyes.

Vince just wanted to hold her and make all the hurt go

away. He took his thumb and wiped the remaining moisture from beneath her eyes. "You're a beautiful woman, Hanna Creed Rosser. Your ex is a moron."

Hanna stood and paced away from him, toward the back of the store. "A moron with a twenty-three-year-old blond law student who looks up to him like he's a king."

Slowly Vince approached Hanna as she straightened a shelf of knickknacks, putting them back in the exact same places they were before she started.

The corners of her bow-shaped mouth turned down. "Thanks for the lovely compliment, Vince. But...that kiss Saturday night was...a mistake."

"I don't see it that way." He moved in closer and wrapped a silky brunette curl around his finger. "As hard as I've tried to stay away this week, not to rush things, I couldn't stop thinking about you. We have something here and you know it."

She leaned her face into his caress. "Yeah, but we're at different places."

Moving closer, he brought his lips to within a hairbreadth of hers. "I think we're at the exact same place. I've just been here a little longer."

Her gorgeous brown eyes searched his for a long moment, then fluttered closed. "Convince me."

He followed her as she backed up against the wall, then cupped her face and took her mouth for a slow, sensuous kiss. "We're both single parents." His lips traveled down her jaw to nuzzle her neck, just where it curved into her shoulder.

She sighed. "Um-hmm." Her tongue touched her lips and her eyes remained closed, her long lashes dark against her creamy complexion.

"Both our lives center around our kids and they get along." He slipped a hand behind her neck and nibbled her ear, breathing in her faint perfume. His other hand glided lower to her bottom.

"True." Her husky voice sounded breathless as she arched her back and pressed against him.

"But as much as we love our kids, we both need adult companionship." He adjusted his position so they were touching full-length and covered her mouth again, deepening the kiss.

She tilted her head back and threaded her fingers through the hair at the nape of his neck. "You're a romantic sort. Direct and to the point."

He slid one hand beneath her shirt and up her torso to cup her breast. "Gotta be specific about what you want or you end up with a green tie with a dopey-looking Santa on it for Christmas."

A smile curved her lips and her eyes slowly opened. "Or a new vacuum with all those snazzy attachments that nobody uses. Figuratively speaking, of course."

Vince winced. "Hope he slept on the figurative sofa that night."

Her smile faded. "Vince, that Southern charm of yours is quite disarming, but I'm not ready for this. The timing just… isn't right."

"At this stage, I'm not suggesting we get married and live happily ever after."

She eased out from between him and the wall. "No. You just need a bed partner."

"You know it's more than that."

"I've only been divorced a month. I am not rushing into another mistake. I can't put Ashton through more drama."

"Hanna, at the risk of sounding crass, spring break is next week. Both kids will be out of town. I'll take you anywhere you want to go."

"And at least three people will call my mother to get the scoop before we're even out of the city limits. When I stopped by for cinnamon rolls this morning, Mrs. Barkley commented that your truck spends a lot of time parked at the bookstore."

"We'll be discreet," he said.

She laughed. "That might be a tad difficult since I live with the queen of the grapevine." She ran her palm down his cheek. "I can't put myself through that."

Vince tried not to grit his teeth. He understood not being ready. Hell, it had taken him nine years to be open to another relationship. How could he expect her to be there straight out of a messy divorce? Yet something felt right with Hanna that he hadn't felt in way too long. "The last thing I want to do is add to your stress." The woman was wound so tight she was about to snap. "I'll back off. I won't pressure you."

"Thank you." It was some consolation that at least she didn't look quite as relieved as he'd anticipated.

"I'm sorry the kids upset you today. And I'm sorry for interfering with the way you're raising Ashton. Once again I'll try to make it clear to Kenzie that Ashton had better get your permission before they do anything else."

Hanna rubbed her forehead. "I appreciate your support. And I realize Ashton is testing his boundaries, testing me and I'm overreacting, taking it out on you. There's anger buried inside Ashton and it's beginning to erupt." Tears swamped her big brown eyes and that tough gravelly voice cracked. "And what scares me is that, if asked, Ashton very well might choose to move back to Dallas with his father."

"I can't imagine. I was forced into single parenthood, but it was just me and Kenzie and we had to figure it out together. Nobody was trying to take her away from me." He twisted a soft curl around his finger. There was a lot of anger and hurt buried in Hanna, too.

Vince left Hanna locking up the shop and loaded Kenzie's bike into the truck bed. His daughter could use a lesson in respect.

The kitchen light was on when he got to the house, but Boo was outside. "What's up, boy?" The mutt nuzzled his hand and loped along behind him into the house.

Vince dropped onto a bar stool and watched Kenzie flounce around the kitchen, giving the dog a rawhide bone, grabbing a soda. "You want one?"

"Yeah." He took the soda she handed him. "Now sit down and let's talk."

Popping the top on her can, Kenzie flipped her ponytail behind her shoulder and took the aggressive approach. "Dad, you see what she does to him. He's not in kindergarten."

"It's not your place or mine to dictate how someone else raises their child. Hanna is doing what she feels is in Ashton's best interest whether you agree or not. And in this case, I happen to agree with her. He should have asked permission before he went fishing. And so should you."

"Sure, and have her tell him he couldn't go. I even told her we had on life jackets and she still went off on us."

Boo took his rawhide and moved a safe distance away. He flopped down in the hall to chew the treat, but his eyes followed every gesture they made.

"Hanna's his mother. She has the right to tell him he can't go."

"Just because she's his mother, that gives her the right to ruin his life?"

"Your attitude needs adjusting. Since you aren't showing that you can be responsible, the bike is off limits until after spring break. One more outburst and I'll call Gran and Pop and cancel the Disney trip for next week."

Kenzie swallowed and her eyes got watery, but she didn't respond.

What they said about disciplining your kid hurting you more than them had never seemed quite so profound, but he'd be damned if he was going to raise a brat. "Mackenzie,

I don't let other people tell me how to raise you. I make the best choices I know how to make, whether they turn out to be the right ones or not. Ms. Rosser does the same. I respect that and I expect you to do the same."

She sniffed. "Yes, sir."

"Now finish your drink and get started on your homework. I've got to make a couple of calls, then I'll start dinner."

Dinner was unusually quiet, and afterwards Kenzie returned to the living room and her homework without being told. Vince was in the middle of loading the dishwasher when Boo's ears perked and he let out a low growl from deep in his throat.

Vince dried his hands and opened the back door to find Ashton, loaded down with a backpack and a little blue overnight bag. "Hello, Mr. Keegan."

"Ashton."

"I was wondering if it'd be okay if I stayed here, at least until Saturday when my dad comes to get me."

Crap. Vince stood back and motioned him in off the dark porch. "You have a home."

Boo plodded over and sniffed Ashton's suitcase as if he expected to find a treat.

Ashton rubbed Boo's head, but didn't seem to get too much relief out of petting the dog. "My home used to be in Highland Park, but now my dad has that girl living there. I go there every other weekend, but last time he worked all day Saturday and she looked at me like she'd never seen a kid before. Then on Sunday we had to go to church, have lunch with my grandparents and then drive and meet Mom in Waco." Misery was etched in frown lines on his forehead and around his downturned mouth.

"What about your new home here? Marble Falls is pretty cool."

"Living with Nana?" He snorted. "She's totally in my

business all the time. I just have this little room and only half my stuff. Mom acts all weird and mad at everything. I didn't have many friends in Dallas, but now they're always busy when I'm there, and Mom screws up the one friend I made here." Ashton tried to act tough, but his dark eyelashes were damp and spiky. "So I just need to stay here until Saturday, if that's okay."

Kenzie slipped quietly into the kitchen. "It's okay if he stays here, right, Dad? It's just two nights."

"Homework, Mackenzie."

"But…" Scowling, she turned and stomped back to the living room.

"Sit down, Ashton. You need a bottle of water or anything?"

"No, thanks. Just a place to stay." The kid deposited his stuff beside the chair and sat. "I can sleep on the sofa."

"Does your mom know where you are?"

"No, she was in the shower when I left."

Vince sat across from him. "Divorce sucks, huh?"

"It sucks green pond scum," Ashton said without even a smirk. "Parents don't care what they do to the kid, they're so busy hating each other."

"I don't know your dad, so I'm not going to speak for him. But your mom is more worried about you and making you happy than anything else right now. You're her whole life. Divorce sucks for her, too."

"Mom says we're living in Nana's home and we have to conform, but I hate it there. I love her, but living with her is not fun."

"You and your mom will get your own place eventually. This is just temporary. Running away from things you don't like isn't going to make them go away."

"You don't know how much it sucks there."

Vince kicked back from the bar and tried to figure out

whether to approach him as a kid or an adult. "When Kenzie's mom and brother were killed, it was just the two of us left. We were both upset and lost and confused. She was only three, but we stuck together. It took a while, and we still just take one day at a time and figure out what works for us. Good or bad, we're a team and we stick together. So are you and your mom. Don't you think she might be worried about where you are?"

"You could call her and tell her I'm staying over. She listens to you."

Yeah, right. "She'd listen to you, if you'd talk to her. Gotta face your problems and be involved in the solution or other people end up making decisions you don't like."

One corner of Ashton's mouth turned up. "So you're telling me to man up?"

"Pretty much. You're old enough and smart enough to do that."

"I'd look more like a man if Mom would let me get a real haircut. She keeps taking me to a salon. Think I might tag along next time you go to your barber?"

"That's just one more thing you need to take up with your mom. She'd skin me alive if I took you for a haircut without her permission."

"So you're scared of her, too?"

"Well, yeah." Vince grinned and picked up the suitcase. "Ready to give it a shot?"

VINCE KEPT HIS HAND ON Ashton's shoulder for moral support and had his finger on the bell when the door burst open and Hanna almost ran them down.

Car keys in hand, no makeup and wild wet corkscrew curls that smelled like shampoo. Old sweatpants and a T-shirt, but no bra.

Staring at him, she blinked, then looked down and her

gaze landed on Ashton. She grabbed him by the shoulders and Vince wasn't sure whether her intent was to shake the boy or kiss him. "Where have you been? I got out of the shower and went in to see how the homework was coming and you were gone."

Ashton leaned away from her, but they were both teary-eyed. The kid didn't respond.

Straightening, Hanna stepped fully out on the porch, closed the door and faced Vince. "What's going on here?"

This was between mother and son, and Vince's intent was to deliver the boy and stay the hell out of it. "Ashton, you going to tell your mom?"

Ashton shrugged, and Hanna finally noticed the blue suit-case and backpack. "You ran away from home?"

"Oh come on, Mom. Don't act so surprised." He shoved past her, lugging his suitcase and backpack. "Thank goodness I'm going to Dad's for a week." The door slammed behind him.

Hanna put her hands on her hips and stared up at the sky. "What next? I can't take this anymore. I don't know what to do."

It took all Vince's willpower not to pull her into his arms. Instead he squeezed her shoulder. "Just one day at a time."

Chapter Eight

Hanna held two pitchers of lemonade high over her head and plastered herself flat against the door frame as three twelve-year-old boys raced out into the yard. It was still five minutes until two, but already six kids from Ashton's class had arrived. In spite of a forecast of possible storms, Saturday had dawned with only scattered clouds for Ashton's birthday party.

She'd debated whether to cancel the party entirely after Ashton's recent disobedience, but hadn't had the heart. Seeing his beaming face as the other kids arrived, she was happy she hadn't. At least he was settling in here. Whether Kenzie's friends or Ashton's, they'd showed up.

She inhaled the sweet scent of the freshly mowed lawn and listened to the squeals of the kids playing dodgeball against the back fence.

"Dad!" Ashton yelled, tossing the ball to another boy and heading toward the patio where Hanna was setting up the refreshments. The fragrance of Richard's cologne preceded him, even before she turned and saw him coming out the sliding glass door.

"Happy birthday, kiddo." Richard gave Ashton's shoulder a squeeze and handed him a huge, beautiful package wrapped in bright-blue foil paper and tied with a shiny silver bow.

"Oh, wow!" Ashton shook it and held it up to his ear as

if he expected it to whisper what was inside. "Can I open it now?"

"We'll open presents later," Hanna said, reaching to take the package. "Let me put that in the house with the others."

"Here, let me get it. It's heavy." Richard touched Hanna's shoulder, then retrieved the present from Ashton.

She flinched at his touch before she caught herself. At least he hadn't brought Phoebe, the new girlfriend. "Thanks. I'm glad you could make the party."

Richard grinned at her, then hauled the gift back inside. They'd agreed to spend special occasions together as a family, for Ashton's sake. It had sounded like a good plan, but this was the first shared event to come up. Maybe it would get easier, but being around him made her jumpy. This was her world, not his. In the years they were together, he'd spent only rare occasions in Marble Falls. Before her father had died three years ago, her parents had typically driven to Dallas for designated holidays. Richard spent so much time at the office, it had just worked out better that way.

"Ashton, the doorbell rang. Better see who it is," Hanna said.

"Let him play. I'll get it," Richard offered, altering his route and heading toward the front door.

The idea was for Ashton to greet his own guests, but Hanna didn't argue. Whatever kept the peace today.

She dumped a bag of chips into a bowl and glanced through the glass door as she heard Vince's deep voice.

Hanna dropped the whole bag in the bowl and bolted into the small living room in time to see Richard extend his hand to Vince. "Richard Rosser, Hanna's—Ashton's father."

"Vince Keegan." Vince shook his hand, but his dimples flashed as he exchanged a knowing glance with Hanna.

Fidgeting by her father's side, Kenzie looked Richard up

and down, then smiled at Hanna. "Hi, Ms. Rosser. Thanks for having me."

"Hi, Kenzie." Hanna blinked at Kenzie in the cute little purple short set, with even a matching bow on her ponytail. Okay. So this must be a twin Mackenzie? "Your hair looks so pretty today. Did you do it yourself?"

Mackenzie crossed her eyes and nodded toward Vince. "I always do it myself. See, he's an engineer and he engineers a ponytail so tight my eyes are on either side of my head."

Vince smirked. "When I put it up, it doesn't fall down, now does it?"

Kenzie smirked at him, then, having fulfilled her mannerly obligation, darted into the yard with the others.

Richard laughed then switched his attention back to Vince. "Have you always lived in Marble Falls?"

"Austin."

Oh, yeah, here came the subtle interrogation. Leave it to Richard.

Richard's gaze quickly took in Vince's faded jeans and white button-down. "Austin. You're not by chance related to Madeline Grant Keegan are you?"

"Guilty." Vince grinned. "My mom."

Well, that slowed Richard down. Hanna'd never seen him look quite so stunned. "At last year's state conference, she gave a hell of a keynote on family law."

"Yeah. Don't mess with Mom."

The hair on the back of Hanna's neck stood up. Having these two men in the same room might not feel awkward to them, but it sure as heck did to her.

Ashton rushed into the living room. "Vince, we're choosing teams for a softball game. Mom bought me equipment for the party. You have to pitch. We decided it's fair as long as you pitch for both teams."

Richard glanced at Vince then took a step toward the back door. "I can pitch a few balls."

Without missing a beat, Ashton grabbed Vince's arm. "Thanks, Dad, but Vince knows how to throw curveballs."

Closing her eyes a second, Hanna prayed Vince would just follow Ashton out and let her deal with Richard. When she opened her eyes, Vince was staring at her.

"Sounds like I've been drafted," he said, rolling up his sleeves and following Ashton.

If looks could kill, Vince would be annihilated by Richard's menacing glare. Without saying a word to her ex-husband, Hanna grabbed the plastic cups and tray of cookies and carted them out to the patio table. Richard followed her outside, slammed closed the ice chest one of the kids had left open and watched the game, hands on hips.

She deposited the stuff on the table and turned to make sure he wasn't going to do anything to ruin Ashton's birthday. She didn't need the two men getting into a macho turf war over who threw the best curveball.

As she turned, Richard grabbed her arm. "Don't try to tell me nothing's going on between you and the cowboy."

She sucked in a breath. "It's not my plan to tell you anything."

He stuffed his hands in his navy blue Dockers and narrowed his eyes at her. She held his stare. No way in hell was she discussing Vince Keegan with her ex-husband. Let him think whatever he wanted.

Slowly he dropped the stare and surveyed the ball game being laid out. "This is how you're raising our son?"

A backyard party certainly hadn't been the norm up until this year. It couldn't compare to trips to the planetarium, laser tag or the gaming arcade that had cost more than she currently cleared in two weeks. But it had been what Ashton had requested and it fit her budget. "Ashton is settling in nicely here. He's made friends. Experienced new things."

She started to turn away, but Richard captured her hand. Obviously he was looking for anything to make his case that Ashton belonged in Dallas. "And education? How's that going? Is he in honors classes? He said he isn't in band. How are his grades?"

Gently she pulled her hand out of his grasp. "There's more to education than just the right schools. There's…"

Hanna risked a glance outside at Vince, then turned and found Richard waiting on her to finish her thought. "I mean, Ashton has come a long way. His three-week report was all A's. Marble Falls has been good for him."

Her gaze was drawn back to Vince and this time that intense blue gaze bored into hers.

Bully Baer put the bat on his shoulder. "You gonna pitch or what?"

Turning his attention back to the game, Vince wound up and threw a curveball over home plate.

Billy missed and put the bat back on his shoulder. "Toss me another one."

"Why? You can't hit worth a flip anyway," Kenzie taunted from second base. Her ponytail was loose and the hair ribbon, no longer in a bow, hung down her back as she flashed her father a wide smile.

Ashton was covering first base. He bent at the waist, spat on his hands and wiped his palms on his jeans. "Let's play ball."

It wasn't his improved athletic skills that touched Hanna, it was his confidence. His assurance. She grabbed her camera off the table and snapped a couple of pictures. His happiness and well-being were all that mattered.

Richard leaned over. "So that's the infamous Mackenzie that I hear all these exaggerated tales about."

"I assure you, tales about Mackenzie require no exaggeration."

Billy made contact with the third ball and it bounced down the first-base line. Ashton rushed to grab it, but Billy raced past first and on toward second. Huffing, Ashton rescued the ball and tossed it to Kenzie, but Billy was halfway to third.

Kenzie tossed the ball to Vince in the pitcher's box and Billy froze on third.

"You'll never make it home, Bully Baer," Kenzie taunted.

As Hanna fidgeted with the refreshment table, Richard frowned. "What if I paid Ashton's tuition? Could you afford a place in Dallas? Put Ashton back in private school? Be closer so I could see him more?"

"Don't start this. We've already uprooted him once this year. I'm not doing it again."

He took her hand and stilled her so she had no choice but to look at him. "I'm no longer first in my own son's life. I can't believe I let this happen."

Not exactly her perception. "Richard, you didn't 'let' it happen, you had an affair. You demanded a divorce. You were the one who was unfaithful, yet you're acting angry as though it was my fault."

Dropping her hand, he looked away. "I felt like an ass, but I couldn't accept that I was to blame, so I lashed out at you. The 'If you'd only been more attentive' defense."

She watched the other team take the field and Ashton's team line up to bat. Clouds were rolling in, but she hoped they'd hold off for a couple of more hours.

Turning back to Richard, she tried to sort out what she was hearing. "You couldn't have just been honest and said that you'd found someone else?"

Now he wanted to have his cake and eat it, too. He wanted

his new young girlfriend, but he wanted Ashton and Hanna close by so he could be a part of Ashton's life.

Squeezing her shoulder, Richard shrugged. "I handled the situation badly. I admit it. But look around. You're too classy for this nowhere town. Ashton doesn't belong here. What if I help you get a bookstore started in Dallas? You'd generate more business than here."

Of all the nerve. "I love my little bookstore here in Marble Falls. And frankly, I have no desire to disrupt my life to make yours easier. You made your choice. Pardon me if I don't really give a shit whether you get to see Ashton."

"What? Now I don't even get to see Dad?"

She hadn't realized Ashton had walked up. How much had he overheard?

"First you moved me to Marble Falls away from him, and now I don't get to see him at all?" Ashton's voice rose with each syllable.

"Ashton…"

"All you two do is yell and fight. You don't care about me at all, just yourselves. Well, fine. I hate you both!"

Ashton's shrill voice silenced the yard. Mackenzie pushed her way through the other kids to her friend and Vince followed.

"You're ruining my life. I was happy in Dallas before the divorce. You said nothing would change, but then you moved me here and said it'd be cool. I was miserable until we met the Keegans and then you tried to forbid me from playing with Kenzie. And you said not to worry, that I could always see Dad, and now you even lied about that."

"Son, calm down," Richard said, reaching for Ashton's shoulder.

"Just leave me alone! I hate you for divorcing us for another woman. And I hate not having a home. And I hate my whole stupid life." Jerking away, Ashton took off down the hall and slammed his bedroom door.

"Ashton!" Hanna raced after him, but he was leaning against the door, preventing her from opening it.

"Go away! I don't want to talk to you."

Hanna's insides were wound so tightly, she wasn't even sure how she could move. "Okay. We can talk later when you aren't so angry."

She turned back toward the living room and found a roomful of little eyes on her. What now? She tried to smile, but her eyes were full of tears.

"Okay, teams." Vince motioned toward the patio door. "Everyone back outside. There are drinks in the cooler and snacks on the table. Five-minute break then get back to the game. Hopefully Ashton will be out shortly."

Hanna flashed him a grateful look.

Mackenzie's eyes were as round as half dollars. She looked at Hanna. "Let me talk to him. Maybe he still likes me okay."

Hanna nodded and Kenzie disappeared down the hall. Vince herded the other kids back toward the yard and closed them outside. Hanna exchanged looks with Vince. If Ashton would listen to anyone, it was Vince's daughter.

"I'll take care of him." Richard took a step.

Vince touched his shoulder. "Might want to let him simmer down a little first. Don't think you're going to get too far right now."

Richard spun on him. "Don't tell me how to handle my son. *My* son. And *my* wife, who, no doubt, you've been sleeping with."

Hanna couldn't just let that one pass. "Ex-wife. And whatever does or does not happen between Vince and me is not your concern."

"It certainly is my concern when it involves my son being

subjected to his mother's sordid affair with his friend's father."
It took a lot to make Richard lose his cool, but Vince had
managed it without even breaking a sweat.

The front door opened and Hanna's mother walked in. She
looked between the three angry faces and froze. "Uh, Anne
Haythorn volunteered to watch the shop for a couple hours
so I could come home and see Ashton blow out his candles.
Did I miss it?"

Hanna shook her head. "No, Mom. We haven't brought out
the cake yet."

"I obviously missed something."

The men didn't even acknowledge Norma, but continued to
glare at one another. Richard looked angry enough, but Vince
could halt an entire room given his current stance. Jaw set,
hands in his jeans pockets.

"I'm going to see about Ashton and Mackenzie." She left
them standing in the living room and knocked on Ashton's
bedroom door. Not a sound. "Ashton." Nada. She opened the
door and peeped inside, but the window was wide open, cur-
tain rustling as the wind picked up.

She raced back into the living room. "They're gone!"

Chapter Nine

Vince blinked and bolted down the hall. Hanna wasn't sure whether he thought she might have overlooked them hiding under the bed.

Thunder rumbled in the distance and the clouds overhead rolled across the sky. That spring storm the weatherman had predicted was moving in. Naturally, this would be the one time a weatherman was right.

Hanna raced after Vince as he ran for the pickup, digging his keys out of his pocket. "Where are you going?"

"Checking to see if the boat's missing. When Kenzie needs to escape, that's her method of choice."

"Oh my God. The wind is picking up and the bottom is going to fall out of those clouds. Surely they wouldn't go out on the lake."

She grabbed his arm and turned, yelling over her shoulder. "Mom, can you get the other kids home safely?"

"I've got it. Just find Ashton," Norma said.

Vince pulled away from Hanna and got in the pickup, but she jumped in beside him, and Richard pushed her over to the center and joined them.

"If anything happens to Ashton..." Richard started.

Hanna glared. "You're right in the middle of this whole insanity, Richard. Don't start making threats."

How much of a head start did the kids have? How much time had they wasted arguing?

Vince took out his cell and dialed. "Kenzie's not answering." He dialed a second number and looked out at the sheet of rain as the clouds opened up. "Hey, Gray, where are you? The kids are missing." Vince paused to listen. "Okay. Can you swing by the house and see if there's any sign of them? Then maybe Bluebonnet Books."

Vince nodded. "Yeah, I'm headed to the folks' house to see if Kenzie's boat is missing." Heavy raindrops pelted the cab but didn't slow Vince down.

Hanna glanced at Richard sitting helplessly beside her. The wipers swished at high speed and still couldn't keep the windshield clear enough to see.

Vince pulled up to the Maguires' dock and got out. The red bicycle. Hanna's stomach plummeted. No kids. And no boat.

"Dammit!" Vince looked out across the lake. Heavy clouds hung low across the choppy water, limiting visibility. "I don't see them."

Bolting out the driver's door, Hanna yelled, "Wouldn't the Maguires have stopped them?"

"They're in Fredericksburg at my brother-in-law's for the week, watching his kids."

Hanna stared across the lake. "I don't think they'd take the boat out in this."

"This moved in so fast, they probably didn't think how bad it was going to get. Even ten minutes ago it didn't look like this." He pulled out the cell again. "Hey, Sheriff, this is Vince Keegan. We've got a problem."

An old rattletrap pickup pulled up beside them, and Gray rolled down the window. "They'd been there. House is unlocked and Boo's gone."

"We wasted too much time," Hanna said, climbing back into the truck cab.

"Two twelve-year-old kids and a big dog. My daughter's small runabout is missing, and I'm figuring she and Ashton took it out on the lake. They were upset." Vince slid behind the wheel and closed the door. He pushed his wet hair back, listening to the sheriff. "Okay. Headed downriver. If you get any reports, you have my cell."

Gray waved. "I'll wait here in case they circle back."

Funny how Vince and Gray anticipated each other's thoughts. Richard hadn't opened his mouth since Hanna had shut him down.

"Where are we going?" Hanna asked as Vince pulled the truck back onto the highway.

"If they're on the water, the wind and waves will take them in this direction. Just watch the lake."

Hanna closed her eyes a second and offered up a prayer for their safety. This could not be happening.

As Vince crept along the lake road, Hanna and Richard kept their eyes peeled for anything on the water, but they could be only twenty feet away in this rain and she wasn't sure they'd see them.

The shrill ringing of Vince's cell phone broke the sound of the rain, and he pulled over to answer it. "Yeah. Okay. How long?" He'd already started moving again and turned up a side road along a cliff. "We're close. See you in a minute."

The truck bumped down a gravel road and Vince squinted through the struggling wipers. "Somebody reported two kids in a boat floating downstream. Watch the water and the shore."

"Look," Hanna screamed. "Isn't that Boo?"

Pulling the truck off the road, Vince slammed it into Park, jumped out and grabbed the huge dog in a hug. "Where are they, boy? Come on."

Ignoring the rain, Hanna raced after Vince as he ran after the dog. Hopefully there would be two wet but alive kids waiting.

"Quiet." Vince put out his hand and stopped Hanna. "Listen."

Richard raced up beside Hanna, but remained quiet.

"Help! Down here. Anybody!" The voice was faint, but obviously Mackenzie's.

"Mackenzie, where are you?" Vince yelled.

Two voices joined in the noise. "Down here. Look over the ledge. Right below the tree."

Vince lay down on his belly and eased out far enough to see over the granite ledge. "Are you both okay?"

"I am. Ash can't walk on his ankle. We tried to climb out and he slipped."

"Just stay where you are. I'll come to you." He went back to the truck and moved it closer, circling around so the back of the truck faced the cliff. He dug a rope out of the bed and tied it securely to the trailer hitch. Tossing the other end over the ledge, he looked at Hanna and Richard. "It's only about a ten foot drop, but it's straight up. I need one of you to get behind the wheel and the other to stand close to the ledge and relay whatever I tell you. When I say pull up, keep your foot on the brake and creep forward as slowly as you can."

Richard jumped behind the wheel. Hanna moved closer to the edge. *Please help Ashton not be hurt.* "I'm here, Ashton. It's going to be okay. You'll be out of there in a minute."

She hoped the two of them would hold it together, but Hanna couldn't even breathe. She held on to the limb of a tree and leaned over so she could see.

Vince grabbed the rope and walked his way down the ledge, holding the rope.

He wrapped the bedraggled little girl in a quick hug and

then pulled Ashton into the mix and hugged him. "You okay?"

"Yeah, just my ankle hurts."

"Okay. Hang tight. Kenzie, you're first. I'm going to tie the rope around your waist, but I want you to hold it and walk your way up like you learned in Girl Scouts. Can you do that?"

There were a few grunts and groans as she made her way up, but soon she scrambled over the edge, then stretched out flat on her belly and peered down at Vince and Ashton. "I made it. But Ash can't walk up with his ankle."

Hanna tried to squelch her panic.

Boo sat beside Mackenzie and licked her face. Hanna rubbed the rain out of her eyes and looked down at Vince. His hair was plastered to his head, water dripping over his forehead.

"Toss the rope back down and stand back. I'm going to tie the rope around my waist, and Ashton is going to hang on to my chest while I walk up. With the extra weight, I need Richard to pull the truck forward very slowly when I say."

Mackenzie untied the rope, dropped it back over and wrapped her arms around Boo.

Hanna's silky pantsuit was muddy and wet, but who cared?

"Tell Richard to put the truck in Drive and ease forward. You and Kenzie stand back in case the rope snaps."

Hanna relayed the message and pulled Mackenzie back.

Mackenzie nodded. "It's not that far down. Dad will get him up."

"He sure will," Hanna said. "Everything is going to be fine."

Don't cry. That'll embarrass Ashton. Hanna swiped at her tears, and realized tough little Mackenzie was doing the same as she leaned back against Hanna.

Inch by infinitely slow inch the rope creaked and popped

as it strained against the cliff. She could hear Vince talking softly to Ashton, but she wasn't sure what he was saying. It didn't matter. They were in this together, and if there was anyone on Earth she trusted in a situation like this, it was Vince.

Hanna focused on the rope and the voices grew louder.

"Almost there. Now as I get to the top, you need to just lean back with me until you feel the ground. Okay?"

Slowly Ashton appeared, and Hanna rushed to him and wrapped her arms around his waist, pulling him onto level ground. She couldn't do anything but sit there in the mud and rock him in her arms like an infant. He clung to her, too emotional to remember to be embarrassed.

Vince hoisted himself up beside Ashton as two police cruisers and an ambulance arrived in a kaleidoscope of flashing lights and screaming sirens.

The emergency lights reflecting off the cloud of heavy fog left the cliff side eerie and mysterious. The situation turned chaotic.

Both kids' clothes were muddy and ripped. Kenzie's hair ribbon just a droopy remnant of the pretty bow. But they were safe.

Mackenzie clung to her father, much like Ashton clung to Hanna. Or was it the parents clinging to the kids? Boo couldn't decide who to lick, and even Hanna got a slobbery tongue up her neck. Having never been comfortable with animals, it was amazing how much love she felt for the stinky wet dog as she wrapped her arms around him. He'd led them to the kids.

Richard, the medics and two officers buzzed around them. Richard ran his hand through Ashton's hair. When a medic asked to examine him, Ashton realized he had an audience and released his hold on Hanna, but he sat beside her as the guy examined his ankle.

"Where are your shoes?" Hanna asked as the medics removed Ashton's dripping sock and exposed a purple-and-red ankle twice the size it should be.

"At the bottom of the lake with the boat. I couldn't swim with them on." He winced as the medic gently rotated his foot.

"Life jackets. Did you have on life jackets?" Hanna demanded.

Vince stood, bringing Mackenzie with him to her feet. He didn't even bother to push back his wet hair. His white shirt was stained and half the buttons were missing or unbuttoned.

"Yeah, we had on life jackets. They're down on the ledge. I can go down and get them," Mackenzie offered.

"No." Vince gave her a nudge. "Wait in the truck. There's a blanket behind the seat."

Boo padded along behind Mackenzie, and Vince squatted down beside Ashton. "You were trying to climb the ledge?"

Vince rested a hand on Hanna's shoulder. His quiet strength felt warm and reassuring. Amazing how much a simple touch could soothe her stress.

Ashton winced as the doctor gently rotated his foot. "We thought we could climb up, and Kenzie probably could have, but she wouldn't leave me. It was slippery and my foot got stuck in a crack between two rocks, so when I fell, it didn't. Then she held me up and I wiggled it out. Is it broken?"

The young medic grinned at Ashton. "I don't feel any broken bones, but we'll need an X-ray when we get you to the hospital. Feel like a ride in an ambulance? If you want, we could even turn on the siren."

Not wanting to let Ashton out of her sight, Hanna climbed into the ambulance with him. There was only room for one parent so Richard reluctantly got back in the pickup with Vince, Mackenzie and the dog.

ONCE THEY WERE ON THEIR WAY to the hospital, Vince called Gray to get him to let everyone know they were safe. The pickup cab was quiet. Richard focused straight ahead on the ambulance. Kenzie huddled in the backseat, wrapped in a blanket and hugging Boo. Vince had never been this upset with her, but he kept it to himself, for now. At least he'd get a chance to deal with her later. He'd never been so frightened. His heart was just beginning to settle back to a normal rhythm.

Gray and Norma arrived at the hospital at the same time as the rest of them.

Norma kissed her grandson on his muddy cheek before they wheeled him into the emergency room.

Gray engulfed Kenzie in a bear hug. Richard's clothes were wet, but in good shape compared to Kenzie's and Vince's muddy, soaked attire. Hanna paced back and forth in front of the emergency room's swinging door, oblivious to the swipe of mud down one cheek and her soggy curls. Her pastel-blue pants and blouse would never come clean.

The air-conditioning and his wet clothes left chill bumps, but Vince couldn't leave until he knew Ashton was okay. The medic tried to check Kenzie out, but she insisted she was fine. The girl had scaled the granite ledge like a pro, so Vince didn't see a need to put her through an exam.

Grayson put a hand on Vince's shoulder. "You found them. Everything is okay."

Letting out a breath, the reality of how close they'd come to losing the kids began to register.

As Kenzie paced by, Vince grasped her arm. "Why the hell did you take the boat out in a storm? Don't you have any common sense?"

Her eyes were full of tears and she looked like a drowned cat, but at the moment, he wanted to shake her as much as hug her.

"Ash was mad because his parents are morons, and we just wanted to get away from all the adults that keep ruining our lives so we took the boat."

"You didn't answer your cell."

Her lip quivered. "Ashton didn't want me to, but when the wind kicked up and the waves were tossing us around, I pulled it out to call you, but the boat rocked and I grabbed to hold on and dropped the phone overboard. Then things got scary. The motor wasn't powerful enough against the wind, and we were going backwards more than forwards and waves were coming in the boat. Then the motor died, and I couldn't get it started so we just drifted. I tried to paddle, but the waves were bigger than the ones at Galveston." She sniffed. "I couldn't do anything and then one wave came over the side and we had lots of water in the bottom of the boat. It sunk and we floated until we could reach the bank."

"I still can't understand how you did not notice the storm moving in." His stomach churned from just the thought of what could have happened.

"Because I was so mad at Ms. Rosser."

"Mad or not, you have to use good judgment."

"I know." Tears trickled down her dirty cheeks leaving mud tracks. "Daddy, I'm so sorry. I was so scared and I didn't know what to do."

Grabbing her, he swung her up—something he hadn't done in years—and held her tight.

She wrapped her legs around his waist and her arms around his neck, burying her head in his shoulder.

Her heart beat against his. He couldn't stand being angry at her, but neither could he let her think what she did was okay. "I love you, Kenzie. Next time, think about what you're doing first."

Her arms squeezed his neck so tightly he could barely

breathe. "I love you, too, Daddy. I'm so, so sorry. Is Ash going to be all right?"

"I doubt he'll even spend the night in the hospital."

Grayson patted his back, and Vince loosened his daughter's hold, letting her slide to the floor.

Kenzie scrubbed her wet face, only smearing the mud more. "I want something to drink."

Vince handed her a couple of dollars and then looked across to where Hanna and Richard stood together.

"She's just a kid, Vince," Gray said as he watched Kenzie disappear down the hall.

"And I was too hard on her?" He massaged his temples. "God, man. I almost lost her, too."

Gray motioned toward a couple chairs and sat down. "I know. And I know how devastating just the thought of what could have happened is right now, but the kids are safe."

"Yeah, but Hanna won't ever forgive me for this one. She's told me all along that I was too lax."

"I'm not so sure Hanna blames you." Gray looked across the room, then back at Vince. "You gonna tell me what's going on or do I get to guess?"

This wasn't the time to get into that with his brother-in-law. "Nothing."

"Uh-huh." Gray stared at him. He wasn't buying a word of it.

Kenzie returned with a soft drink and eyed Vince warily. He held out his arms, and she leaned back against him, taking his hands and hugging them across her belly.

"It's okay, Kenzie. Everything's going to be fine." Squeezing her tight, he wondered how much longer she'd let him do that before she grew too old for hugs.

A nurse came through the swinging doors, and Hanna, Richard and Norma followed her down the hall.

Vince left Kenzie with Gray and went to the men's room.

He looked in the mirror and scrubbed his hands up and down his face only to realize they were still shaking. He tried to wash some of the caked mud off his face and hands to at least be a little more presentable.

Kenzie met him at the door, anxious to go check on Ashton. He gave the Rossers a few minutes of family time then went to the receptionist's station. "Is Ashton Rosser allowed to have visitors?"

She checked the computer. "He's just waiting to be released. Emergency room four, just down this hall on the right."

Holding Kenzie's hand, he led the way down the hall and knocked on the door. "Ashton, up to a couple of more visitors?"

The kid was propped up in bed, his ankle elevated on two pillows. "Hey, Vince. Come on in."

Kenzie was sheepish, so Vince walked in ahead and gave the ankle a once-over. "That's some injury you've got there, pal."

"Isn't it cool? It's purple and red and even a green stripe right there. They stitched this up here where the rock ripped the skin. I got to watch. The doc said the scar won't be too bad."

"No biggie. Girls love guys with scars."

Ashton wrinkled his nose. "You think? I can't practice baseball for a week or two."

Kenzie eased up beside Vince, grasped his hand and looked at Ashton's trophy ankle. "I'm sorry I almost got you drowned."

"If it'd just been me, then I'd have drowned. We didn't drown because you made me wear my life jacket and because Boo swam to shore and climbed out and got Mom and Vince."

"So you're really okay?"

"Sure. Look at my foot. It's like twice the size of the other one." He beamed as if having a sprained ankle somehow gave him passage into coolness.

"May not be so fun when the painkillers wear off," Richard said.

Hanna met Vince's eyes and offered a tentative grin, but she remained on the other side of the bed beside Richard. This was a family deal, and he wasn't family. "Kenzie, we should get you home and into dry clothes."

Hanna stepped around the bed. "May I talk to you a minute first?"

Here it comes. Vince left Kenzie sitting on the corner of Ashton's bed expounding about their experience and followed Hanna into the hall and to the window at the end of the corridor where it was quiet. He stared out at the pouring rain and waited. Waited for Hanna to yell about how his lazy parenting style had almost cost her Ashton. Or for her to tell him that she wanted him and Kenzie out of her life.

When Hanna actually touched Vince's shoulder, he jumped. "She's just a child, Vince. It wasn't Kenzie's fault. Or yours."

"I shouldn't have given a twelve-year-old so much freedom."

"And if you hadn't taught her to think for herself, we might be planning two funerals right now instead of just dealing with a sprained ankle and sunken boat." She eased around beside him and caught his attention. Tears glistened on her lashes. "Look at me."

He shoved his hands into his pockets and turned back to the window. Away from her hurt. "If I'd have been stricter with her, she'd have known better than to take the boat out. I gave a kid credit for having adult judgment."

"Mackenzie is a little tenacious, but this little debacle was instigated entirely by Ashton." Hanna flicked a tiny crust of mud off Vince's neck. "Kenzie's ability to think under pressure probably saved both their lives."

"But I gave her too much leeway to do so. Not so smart."

Hanna shrugged. "Agreed. There should be a happy medium."

He stared out the window at the dark clouds and rain, and then turned. He had to see her. Placing both palms on the windowsill behind him, he leaned his weight on them and stared into that gorgeous, muddy face. Even on the rafting trip, Hanna had maintained a classy, together look. He grinned at the mud stains on her expensive outfit and the smudge on the right side of her nose. "Yeah. I'm gonna work on that."

There were still tears in her eyes, but she returned his grin. "All we've heard since we walked into Ashton's room is how you hoisted him up that cliff. If you weren't his hero before, you sealed it this afternoon."

It had been nine years since he'd felt this helpless. His common sense still told him he was raising Kenzie right, but the emotional dad who'd almost lost a child wasn't buying it. "I'm not a hero."

"Maybe not. I still don't agree with the amount of leeway you give Kenzie. But Vince, without her ability to think on her feet and your fast actions, I'm not sure we'd have found them."

He tilted his head and tried to read her. "Is Ashton still going home with his dad tonight?"

"Sounds that way. As long as the doctor releases him in time."

Vince ran a thumb under her eye to dry the tear and only succeeded in smearing the mud. "And your little boy is hurt and you don't want to be apart from him?"

The corner of her bow-shaped mouth turned up. "You know me too well." She massaged her forehead. "God, I need a break. I need a couple of days of total freedom from single

parenting and meddling mothers and controlling ex-husbands. I need to get a grip. I need sleep."

"With ya there. After today, I just want to crawl in bed and sort it all out. Or not think about fatherhood at all. I don't know."

Her dark, sad eyes glistened with unshed tears. She stared at him a good two minutes. "Spring break is next week."

He nodded.

"Convince me we'll be discreet."

Chapter Ten

Tuesday morning, Hanna pulled her Volvo into the small parking lot across from the San Antonio River Walk hotel where she and Vince had arranged to meet. She hadn't actually seen him since Saturday evening when he'd left the hospital, and they'd only found time for a couple of phone calls to plan their getaway.

What if he'd backed out?

She glanced at her cell phone for the umpteenth time, but there were no missed calls or text messages. Not from Vince and not from Ashton.

Vince had spent Sunday in Austin, replacing Kenzie's cell phone and driving her and his parents to the airport for their flight to Disney.

Hanna had spent extralong hours at the shop Sunday and Monday, putting everything in order so her mother couldn't complain about her neglecting her duties. Hanna was in her mid-thirties and really shouldn't let her mother stress her out like this. She and Vince were only going to be gone two days and one night, but she wanted to minimize the flack.

As much as she hated to admit it, her mom was better at knowing what the customers wanted than she was anyway. Mom knew the locals' favorite writers, and when new books were hitting the shelf. She was a wealth of information on local history and activities for the tourists. Hanna's strong point was keeping the financial end of things straight. Boring accountant, divorced single mom. How depressing was that?

She glanced at the hotel. Surrounded by more opulent high rises, it was a quaint little four-story brick building nestled in the towering hundred-year-old live oaks. A splashing fountain added a welcoming touch to the circular brick courtyard. Hanna smiled. The hotel had the same classy, weathered appeal as Vince. Vince. What was she going to do if Vince wasn't inside waiting for her? He might have changed his mind, decided that two days away wasn't worth the risk of the kids finding out.

Steeling herself against further panic, Hanna grabbed her overnight case and locked the car. He wouldn't do that to her.

She shouldered her purse and slid her sunglasses on top of her head to keep the wind from blowing her hair in her face. Pulling her little roller bag behind her, she started toward the hotel entrance.

This escape had disaster written all over it. What if they ran into someone from Marble Falls? She stopped. She should just get back in the car and drive as fast and far away as she could. She took another step forward. This escape might just save her sanity.

The heavy glass door swung open as she approached and refreshing air cooled her face. She looked around the plush lobby. Beautiful silk flower arrangements and leather sofas you could bury into. A polished wood reservation desk. Small but classy.

As she recognized Vince slowly walking toward her, she let out her breath. No man had ever looked as good as he looked to her in his familiar faded jeans and black shirt. That lazy smile and the crinkles at the corners of those denim-colored eyes. He kissed her cheek. "I planned to play the Southern gentleman and at least meet you at the car."

Shivering in the air-conditioned room, she released her roll-along bag and wrapped her arms around him, tilting her face up for a real kiss. "You have two whole days to practice."

He encased her in a full bear hug, then, keeping an arm around her, grabbed the handle of her bag, escorting her toward the elevators.

The clerk behind the counter smiled as they passed, and welcomed her to San Antonio. People roamed about the lobby and a young man and woman herded two small, swimsuit-clad preschoolers toward the pool.

Riding up in the elevator, Hanna's stomach fluttered like springtime butterflies in the Hill Country. She glanced at Vince standing beside her and sucked in her breath. She'd never in her life done anything this spontaneous and irresponsible.

But never before had she been this emotionally drained and in need of something for herself. Something that she wasn't doing for her husband. Or for her son. Or for her mother. Or because it was the proper and expected thing for her to do.

She turned as Vince touched her shoulder and the elevator doors glided silently open. She tried to still the butterflies. She'd never spent the night in a hotel with any man other than Richard. And they'd been married.

Vince inserted the card key and stood back for her to enter.

Grasping her small yellow purse, Hanna stepped into the room, and, in spite of the balcony and view of the river, her gaze landed on the king-size bed piled with assorted pillows and shams. This was far from a bargain-priced room.

Vince hoisted her bag up beside his leather duffel on the bureau. Averting her eyes from the bed, she opened the French doors onto the balcony and stepped out.

Two wrought-iron chairs and a round table decorated the semi-circular balcony. Trees reached as tall as their third-floor balcony, giving it a cozy, natural feel. Hanna leaned over the wrought-iron rail and waved at the water taxi that putted by on the river below. A couple strolling arm-in-arm along the sidewalk waved back along with the people on the boat.

Vince stepped up behind her and placed both hands on her shoulders. "What do you think? Good enough for a getaway?"

"Perfect. All the times we drove through town when I was a kid, we never came down to the river."

"You grew up an hour and a half from the River Walk and never came here? Now that is amazing."

"Mom didn't like the humidity on the water."

Vince wrapped his arms around her stomach and nuzzled her neck. "Humid or not, it's one of the most romantic destinations in Texas."

"Romance. Not Mom's strong suit. Or I don't think it was anyway."

Turning her head, Hanna met Vince's lips. "Just for tonight. Let's pretend we don't have mothers." She tilted her head, stared into his eyes, then covered his lips with hers. "Or kids or ex-husbands."

He sucked her bottom lip into his mouth. "Right there with you."

Hanna felt the slight trepidation in his kiss. Was he as nervous as she was about this? He wound one dark curl around his finger and stared at her mouth. "Ready to experience the Mercado? Make lunch an adventure."

"Uh, sure." That husky voice of his was sexy as hell. She'd heard of bedroom eyes, but he had a bedroom voice.

"You said you wanted a Southern gentleman," he drawled as he took her hand and looked wistfully at the king-size bed.

She smiled. There was always tonight. Before she changed her mind and decided just to go for it, Vince led her out of the room and locked the door with the bed safely behind them.

It was late morning as they strolled through the Mercado Mexican market to see what goodies they could find to snack on as they shopped. It felt good to stretch her legs and not to worry about whether Ashton was entertained. They bought some trinkets for the kids and grabbed sodas and a paper container of nachos to tide them over until dinner.

The Mercado was crowded, but it was exciting to wander through and check out all the vendors, food and clothes. Hanna enjoyed the feel of her hand in Vince's as they browsed and people-watched. She wasn't interested in buying so much as just checking things out.

They tried on hats in one store and Vince even modeled a sombrero. By the time they finished their tour, they were both tired, so they bought two passes for the river taxis.

HOLDING HANNA'S ARM as she stepped into the flat boat, Vince tried to put sex out of his mind. But the sway of her jeans-clad bottom as she walked in front of him and selected a spot on one of the benches wasn't working in his favor.

She was tall for a woman and slender, but there was nothing fragile about Hanna Creed Rosser. She hid her strength beneath classic clothing and that gravelly voice, but it was there. Hanna bounced back from adversity with the same determination as her sexy dark curls bounced back when pulled.

She could take care of herself. Which was why he was flattered by her eagerness to escape responsibility for a couple of days with him. They both needed this.

Hanna seemed content to lean back against his arm and just take it all in as they made their way down the various forks in the river, passing other hotels, outdoor restaurants and expensive shops. "See anywhere you want to check out, just speak up."

Nodding, she pointed to a pigeon perched on the beams under a bridge as they cruised beneath it. The taxi driver, an older Hispanic gentleman wearing a black-and-white-striped shirt, tossed out tidbits of San Antonio history as they toured different areas of the river.

Vince moved to the bench opposite Hanna and pulled out his camera. When he lined her up on the screen, he found that she had her own camera, taking his picture as he took hers. "Trying to be funny, woman?" After a few shots he moved back beside her and another passenger reached for Vince's camera. "Allow me."

They snuggled close for another shot.

The chime of Vince's cell phone interrupted the tour and he glanced at the readout. "Hey, Kenzie. Having fun?"

"Oh, Dad, it's a blast. Not as much fun as when you came with us before, but we spent today at the water park and yesterday we rode every roller coaster at Disney—Space Mountain twice. And you should see the pool at the hotel!"

"Cool. You minding Gram and Pop?"

"Yeah, they're having fun, too. Sorry you're missing Pop's purple-flowered swim trunks. Whoa. I had to put on my sunglasses."

"Don't forget the sunscreen, okay? Remember last time."

"I know. Gram slathered it all over me twice already. I feel like a greased pig. Gotta go. Pop just came back with hot dogs."

"Love you, Kenzie. Be good." He slid the phone back into his pocket.

"Sounds like she's having a good trip."

"She has my parents wrapped around her finger. Leo and I never got away with half of what she does."

"And I thought Ashton's grandparents spoiled him. But they mostly buy him things. They're quiet people. Not sure they'd survive spring break in an amusement park full of hyper kids. I just wish Ashton would call. I'd like to hear his voice, you know?"

"So call him. Bet he'd like to hear your voice, too."

The corners of her mouth turned down. "He's with his dad, and I don't want to interfere. We'll talk when he gets home."

So much for not thinking about the kids. Then again, Vince could call Kenzie whenever he wanted. He didn't have to share custody or worry about the ex factor.

Hanna pointed across the river. "Look at all those shops. I'll bet I couldn't afford a thing down here anymore."

Vince motioned to the driver and gave Hanna a kiss. She didn't look nearly as excited as she was trying to sound. Vince took her hand and helped her out of the boat. "Browsing is free."

"True."

In the second shop, Hanna pushed her sunglasses up on top of her head and eyed a bright floral sundress. She looked at some other items, but came back to finger the fabric and check the price tag.

"Try it on." His blood pumped just picturing how she'd look in that feminine little number.

"Nah, I have no place to wear a sundress these days."

"Doesn't cost anything to dream." He leaned around and whispered in her ear. "Do it for me."

With a grin, she selected her size, handed Vince her purse and allowed the saleslady to show her to a dressing room.

He watched the people stroll by as he waited, but when Hanna came out, he couldn't see anything but her. The bodice clung to her like a second skin, the deep V showing off enough cleavage to make his mouth water. Not that she was busty, but she had nice curves. The saleslady picked up a pair of sandals with bright-colored straps and held them up for her approval.

"The heels are too high. I'd look like the jolly floral giant."

Vince took the shoe. "I like 'em. They sorta look like rainbows."

"They are cute."

The saleslady asked Hanna's size and selected a box from beneath the display.

While Hanna sat on a padded bench to try them on, her cell rang. She grabbed her phone as the saleslady buckled the strap on the second shoe. "Tiffany, what a surprise." Her face lit up and she continued to listen as she stood and checked out her reflection in the floor-length mirror. The full skirt moved seductively as she turned for a side view. "Really. They were having lunch at the club? I'm so happy Richard took time off to spend time with him. Ashton needs that reassurance right now."

She became even more animated as the conversation progressed. God, she looked amazing. The dress, the smile, the way those ridiculously high heels made her legs look endless. Maybe she'd be okay with skipping dinner and just hopping a taxi back to the hotel? No, he'd told himself. This trip was for her, and he wasn't going to blow it by rushing things.

"Oh, I miss you all desperately. Just the other day I was thinking about that bread at Kirby's and their wonderful salad."

Vince handed the saleslady his credit card. "Just put the jeans and sneakers in the bag."

"Oh my gosh, you're kidding. Did she really?" Hanna's laughter filled the shop. "So what did he do? Did she get the car?"

The saleslady collected a pair of scissors from the counter and touched Hanna's arm, then gently cut the tags off the dress.

Hanna jerked around, saw the credit card and mouthed at him. "You can't buy this. It's outrageous."

He flashed his best grin and ignored her protest.

122 Second Chance Dad

"A Jag! Oh man, he must have realized how bad he screwed up to spring for a convertible."

Vince signed the credit receipt and took the bag, winking at the clerk. "Thanks."

The wistfulness for her old life was clear in every syllable. It was painted across Hanna's face like a mural. He thought back to the house he'd sold in Austin before moving Kenzie to Marble Falls. A house he'd hoped would make his young wife happy. He'd stretched their resources to buy the place, but he'd been making good money and along with Belinda's teacher's salary, they'd managed.

Although Austin's lifestyle was more laid-back and centered on music than Dallas's country-club culture, Marble Falls had still been an adjustment. It had taken a while even though he'd made the move willingly. But returning to Marble Falls and into the house with her mother probably wasn't a life Hanna would have chosen if there were other options.

He placed his hand on the curve of her back and felt her slim waist beneath the silky fabric. Why did he feel the urge to protect her? The woman would resist him at every step if he even hinted that was his intent.

She took her purse from him and met his eyes. "Listen, Tiffany, I've gotta run. Thanks for reporting in on Ashton. I try not to worry, but it's hard, especially with his sprained ankle. Please don't be a stranger. I love keeping up on the latest. Not as good as being there, but it helps."

Vince slipped his arm around Hanna as they walked out of the store and down the River Walk. "You miss Big D, don't you?"

"I miss my life in Dallas terribly. My house. My friends. Most of the women I ran around with stopped calling after the divorce. I guess Richard got the friends in an unwritten codicil to the divorce decree, huh?"

Ouch. With friends like that... At least she didn't mention

missing her ex-husband. "I miss Austin every so often. But a weekend there usually takes care of that."

The corner of her mouth turned up. "Nice place, but you wouldn't want to live there?"

"Not anymore. It was a great place to grow up and UT was a trip." He turned and walked backwards so he could look at her. The dress left her shoulders bare and her legs. Those heels should be sold in one of those sexy, how-to-seduce-a-guy stores.

She fished her sunglasses from the tangle of curls on top of her head and slid them back on her nose. "At least you chose to move to Marble Falls."

AFTER DINNER AT A SMALL outside table beside the river, they decided against the river taxi in lieu of walking off the heavy enchiladas and margaritas.

Hanna rubbed her stomach and stared at Vince. "That was an amazing dinner, but I probably gained at least three pounds."

He swung the shopping bag in one hand and took her hand with the other. "You can't come to San Antonio without eating Mexican food, though. Trust me, in a week your mouth will start watering and you'll lie in bed dreaming about salty chips and salsa."

Replaying the day, Hanna had no doubt that it was Vince and not just the amazing cuisine that had drawn Hanna in. Her relaxed state had more to do with him than the slushy margaritas they'd consumed with dinner. She dropped his hand and slid her arm around his waist. "Thanks for this."

The sun had set and the River Walk came alive. Tiny white lights twinkled in the trees along the sidewalk and neon flashed from restaurants. Old-fashioned streetlamps illuminated the arched stone bridge that spanned the river. The walkways had become crowded with slower-paced tourists.

Strolling in rhythm to the music of a floating mariachi band on one of the taxis, Hanna couldn't keep from dancing. A small band set up outside a steakhouse cranked out country music. The music, conversation and river taxis' engines melded and overloaded her senses. Hanna had never been anywhere like this.

Vince set the shopping bag against the stone wall and silently pulled her into his arms and into the crowd of country dancers. There were a few others dancing and she willingly melted against him. Being in his arms felt about as right as anything had in years. She buried her fingers in the little curls at the nape of his neck, damp from the humidity. The sexy little sundress made her feel pretty and feminine. And heels. She actually had on three-inch heels for the first time in fourteen years. And even wearing them, she felt small and feminine in Vince's arms.

As the song changed, he fell into the Texas two-step and Hanna tried to follow. He had the steps down to an art. He was good, amazingly good to have just learned a couple of weeks ago in Gruene. Suddenly she froze; a lump lodged in her throat as reality set in. Tears swamped her eyes. "You already knew how to dance the other night? Yet, you let Ashton teach you because you knew how much he needed that."

Hanna's heart melted into a puddle at her feet. Vince had let Ashton "teach" him because he'd realized that the boy needed to feel good about knowing something others didn't. That might not have been a huge deal to any other kid, but to her son, who was struggling in every aspect of his life, it had been a wonderful boost to his ego.

She rested her cheek against Vince's shoulder and felt his heart beat against hers, completely forgetting the steps. As much as she'd tried to resist getting emotionally involved, he'd drawn her in. She'd never met a man like him.

Thunder rumbled off in the distance. "Vince."

"Hmm?" he said, resting his chin on top of her head.

"We should go back to the room."

Chapter Eleven

Vince pulled back and smiled that lazy smile of his. The next moment he was kissing her, his lips hot and full of seductive promise.

He collected her shopping bag and flagged a water taxi as a flash of light illuminated the sky.

Hanna snuggled into the crook of his arm as they chugged along beneath the twinkling lights. The boat's vibration had nothing on the bubbling anticipation she felt in her heart.

Which was ridiculous. She was a thirty-four-year-old divorced woman, not some virgin on her wedding night. Yet she felt jittery and her palms were sweating.

Lightning flashed across the night sky and a deep rumble of thunder chased it down the river. The air felt heavy with the smell of rain. Wind rustled the trees that draped over the river and she buried into Vince's warmth.

She was ready to get to the room and off this water. But the boat continued slowly along, stopping to pick up and let off riders. Their hotel must be the final stop.

"Spring in Texas," Vince said as the water taxi finally glided up to their hotel. He handed the driver a folded bill and took Hanna's arm to steady her as she stepped out of the boat. Huge drops of rain spattered the sidewalk as they raced into the hotel lobby.

Except for the rain pelting the windows, the lobby was

as quiet as if they were isolated, alone. The rest of the world didn't exist.

Vince's shirt clung to his skin, outlining his sculptured chest. She shivered at the goose bumps on her damp skin from the air-conditioned lobby.

Vince scrubbed his hands up and down her arms and their gazes met. The hunger in his eyes matched hers as he took her hand and headed for the elevator.

As soon as the elevator doors shut, Hanna turned and wrapped her arms around his neck, pulling him closer for a kiss. With a rough groan, he covered her lips with his, sliding his hand down her back to cup her bottom. They couldn't get to the room fast enough, and he handed her the shopping bag while he dug the key card out of his wallet and opened the door.

Happiness and nervousness merged and frothed up inside her. This romantic little getaway was totally out of character for her, yet it seemed so right. Almost as if she was just now discovering her true character.

She dropped the bag beside her yellow duffel and reached to remove the wet dress, but Vince was already behind her, his hands at her shoulders. He bent his head to kiss the sensitive skin below her ear. His warm lips felt exquisite against her chilled skin as he slid his fingers beneath the straps and eased the fabric down her arms. Stepping out of the dress, she shivered in only her bra and panties.

She heard his boots hit the floor beside her dress and then the rustle of his shirt joining them. Leaning her head back against his chest, she craved the touch of his skin. The heat from his chest seared into her back.

They'd not bothered to turn on the light, but the drapes over the patio doors were open, and the lightning flashed through the glass like a strobe.

Hanna turned to stare as Vince stepped back and reached

for the snap on his jeans. With a smile, she brushed his hands away and took over the task, enjoying the warmth in his touch as he leaned forward and stole her breath away with another kiss. One hand cupped each side of her face as he deepened the assault.

She slid the zipper down and pushed the jeans over his lean hips, exposing tighty whiteys that were more tight than decent at the moment. Running her hands up his chest while he stepped out of the soft denim, her heart raced. His skin burned beneath her fingers as she tilted her face up, starved for another kiss, desperate for his body against hers.

There was only a second of shyness before Vince waltzed her to the bed and pulled the blanket over them. "Come here."

She snuggled against him, reveling in his hot flesh as he rolled her beneath him and covered her mouth, his kisses deep and greedy. Large hands cupped her satin-clad bottom and held her tight against his long, masculine body. "Warming up?"

She rubbed her hands up his back and thrust them through his rain-dampened hair. "You tell me." Even in the dark, his eyes bored into hers. She relaxed into the soft pillows, enjoying his weight. Enjoying his closeness. And, whoa, those full lips and insane kisses.

Rain peppered the French doors, accompanied by a bright flash of lightning and then thunder so intense the windows rattled.

But the intensity of the storm held nothing to the passion of the man in her arms.

As he slid her panties off, her hands explored his buttocks and legs, taking his tighty whiteys with them. Oh yeah, there was something to be said for a man who didn't earn his living behind a desk. She thought of Richard for a brief second, then

Vince was touching her, caressing her, making her forget... forget...whatever it was she'd been thinking about.

Rubbing her hands down his arms as he rose, she sighed as his muscles flexed and tightened. He rolled away and the bedside drawer creaked open, then she heard the tear of cellophane. She giggled.

He'd told her not to worry about anything. That he'd take care of all the details.

Welcoming him back into her arms, Hanna ran her hands down his shoulder blades, thrilled at how well his body fitted against hers.

Vince groaned and moved lower, kissing her right breast and sliding one hand down her abdomen and between her thighs. His tongue circled her nipple and drew it into his mouth.

Instinctively she arched her back as his fingers penetrated her, sighing in contentment.

"You have a gorgeous body." He kneaded her breast and kissed his way down her stomach. Lightning flashed through the window and she smiled. She had a beautiful body? Vince was an Adonis.

He adjusted his position and brought his lips back to hers. Hanna couldn't get close enough fast enough.

Wrapping her legs around his hips, she slanted her mouth over his and almost purred in ecstasy as they came together.

He seemed to enjoy her participation as they moved in unison, the thunder and lightning barely noticeable compared to the tempest that exploded between them.

It had been years since she'd felt as totally feminine and desirable as she felt in Vince's arms.

Slowly she drifted back to earth and relaxed against him. Smiling in contentment, she ran a hand down his chest, letting the hairs thread through her fingers. "So, what are we going to do if it's still raining tomorrow?"

"What are you worried about? You have a car. I'm down here on the bike." His lips trailed kisses around her jaw and he gently nipped with his teeth. "Still, an excellent excuse not to leave the room all day."

VINCE WOKE SOMETIME during the night with his right arm tingling. Hanna lay snuggled against him, one bare leg thrown across his, an arm across his chest and her head nestled into his shoulder. Pretty comfy, except his arm was numb. He eased her head up, her dark curls tickling his left hand, then slid his right hand from beneath her and placed her head on the pillow.

She was like a cuddly kitten. Playful and fun, yet there were claws waiting beneath the surface if he got out of line. He hadn't been sure what to expect from this trip. More reluctance, maybe.

He picked up one curl and watched it corkscrew around his finger. She worried about the gossip grapevine, yet she hadn't let that sway her from this trip. Obviously Marble Falls wasn't where she wanted to be, but that's where she'd landed to pick up the pieces after her divorce. And since she'd opened Blue-bonnet Books, he could only surmise she planned to stay.

The storm from the night before had settled into a spring rain, and he perhaps had settled into a relationship of sorts. At least, he wanted more than just a hot and heavy trip down the river. It had been nine years since Belinda's death, maybe it was time to move on. He was tired of not having a woman in his life.

He rolled over on his back and closed his eyes. Had he been looking for more from a relationship than a temporary good time? Mrs. Haythorn and even Hanna's mother had hinted for years that he was looking for a mother for Kenzie, or should be. They'd even kept him apprised of any newly single women in town. And twice lately Mrs. Haythorn had brought up how attractive Hanna was. But he had Kenzie under control, and adding a stepmom into that mix could go over like a lead brick. No, what he only now realized was that he was looking for a partner.

He rolled over and watched Hanna rub her eyes and stretch. The sheet fell to her waist, and he trailed a finger from her belly button upwards and palmed her breast. Maybe they could stay all week.

One dark eye opened and she smiled. "Exactly what do you have in mind this early?"

Rolling her on top of him, he started a slow seduction of her lips. Soft, dark curls surrounded her face, brushed against her neck and forehead, and into her eyes. Hanna had no clue how disheveled and cute she looked as she leaned down for another kiss. "The sun isn't even up."

He massaged her back and adjusted her against him. "But I am."

THE SKY WAS STILL GRAY when Vince crawled out of bed, took a quick shower and put the coffeepot on. Leaving Hanna snuggled beneath the covers, he slipped into his jeans and T-shirt and padded barefoot to the elevator. They needed sustenance. Once downstairs, he loaded a tray with croissants, bacon and glasses of juice from the buffet breakfast.

By the time he returned, Hanna was coming out of the bathroom looking sexy as hell in nothing but a hot little yellow negligée. How was a guy supposed to concentrate on breakfast? He placed the tray on the bed and tossed beside it a worn copy of a celebrity rag that someone had left downstairs.

Picking up the magazine, she cocked an eyebrow.

He shrugged. "Thought there might be something in there about Elvis."

Laughing, she dropped it on the nightstand. "You think it's funny that the town gossip's daughter reads tabloids?"

"Sort of."

"I guess the apple doesn't fall far from the tree after all." She didn't look too upset by the discovery.

He leaned in and gave her a quick kiss. "It's charming."

She wrinkled her nose and filled two cups with coffee. "We could eat on that little table by the window."

"Or we could crawl back in bed and eat here." He winked.

Setting the coffee on the nightstand, she eyed him suspiciously. "Vince, I'm really hungry."

He shucked his jeans and propped the pillows up against the headboard. "Me, too."

Without further argument, she joined him. "Breakfast in bed, huh? Always seemed awkward and messy, but hey, this is my time to live dangerously."

Vince wondered if he needed to go down for another tray as they devoured every last crumb he'd brought up. He reached into the bedside drawer and handed her a small box of caramel chocolates. "Dessert."

Licking her lips before she even got the crinkly cellophane off, she opened the shiny gold box. "Chocolate for breakfast! Don't tell my mom."

"After all this, it's the chocolate you're worried about keeping from her?"

Selecting a rich chocolate morsel, she placed it between his lips. "Oh, she had you figured out way before this trip."

He fed her a chocolate in return. "She did, did she?"

"Um-hmm," Hanna said, setting the box on the nightstand and licking a dribble of sticky caramel off her bottom lip. "That was amazing," She looked out at the rain. "I dread going home today."

He took both cups and set them aside. "You worry too much, woman."

"I probably haven't worried enough the past two days.

Facing my mother won't be pleasant, and I hope she's all we have to deal with."

He leaned back against the pillows and she curled into his side, resting her head against his chest.

"Your mother and her grapevine of gossips can only make you as miserable as you allow them to."

"I'm just a bored housewife who couldn't even manage to keep my marriage together. Unlike you—the loving husband who lost a wife and child. They're sympathetic toward the horror you went through."

A lump blocked Vince's throat and the nine-year-old nightmare resurfaced. She couldn't know how much guilt he'd felt—still felt—over the accident. He stood and paced over to the window to stare out at the drizzle. "You don't have the market cornered on guilt."

"Vince, they died in a car accident. There was nothing you could have done to prevent that." Hanna stayed in bed, but her voice penetrated his soul.

"Right! Hell, I was at work. Couldn't have been my fault."

"Vince, I'm sorry." Hanna bolted off the bed and came up behind him. "Bringing that up was totally insensitive of me. I didn't think. I can't imagine how devastating losing your wife and son must have been."

He walked back, sat on the edge of the bed and pulled on his jeans, needing to feel less vulnerable, less…exposed. "Belinda was my best friend. But…when she told me she was pregnant, I thought my life was over. I acted like an ass."

Sitting beside him on the bed, Hanna didn't speak. He expected her disgust, but she just waited. He'd never opened up about this to anyone and he wasn't sure he was ready to now. Hell, he could go to his grave and still not be ready.

"See, I had a plan for my life. I was going to get my Masters in Engineering and Design, and the world was going to be my playground. I was going to design these masterpiece bridges, work all over the world and people were going to stand in awe." He huffed. "A wife and kid didn't fit into my plan, at least not until I had my career together. I figured maybe when I was forty."

Hanna slid her hand down his cheek. "Vince, having a dream is nothing to feel guilty about. Having it taken from you hurts."

"Belinda knew my dream, knew I wasn't ready to get married. Told me to go on with my life. Said her family would be there for her and that she didn't need anything from me. Left campus and headed home to Marble Falls."

Hanna shook her head. "I'm sure you aren't the only guy who wasn't thrilled with that kind of news."

"I stalked around my apartment for a day or two, just wanting her and the baby to…go away…not to exist. Then I went to Marble Falls and met her folks. Apologized to Belinda for acting like a jerk and asked her to marry me."

Hanna touched his arm but didn't comment.

God, he couldn't do this. But when she looked at him like that, he couldn't stop. He needed her to know the truth. "I honored my commitment. When we got married, I was in it one hundred percent. I had a wife and a baby and I did everything I was supposed to do, plus I worked on my Masters at night. We gave the marriage our all. She wanted a home, I worked overtime and bought her a house. She wanted a second child and we had Kenzie. She wanted a perfect family picture on the Christmas card, no problem."

Hanna wrapped the sheet around his bare shoulders and offered him the warmth of her body. "But?"

"Belinda was a hell of a woman. I think I loved her from the day we met. Growing up with four brothers, she understood me too well. I couldn't get away with anything with her." He grinned, remembering the way she'd always had his number.

"We thought alike. There were no bullshit games. Yet she could be totally feminine when she decided to be. The only problem was that I wasn't ready to be married. Then, about the time it penetrated my thick skull that being married to my best friend was a pretty sweet deal, they were gone. Ironic, huh?"

"Not your fault."

"After all, wasn't that what I'd wanted in the beginning?" He forced his fingers to unfist. "She hated freeways. She was a small-town girl and Austin traffic freaked her out. I knew that. She didn't even like to ride with me on I-35, much less drive. So that day I was supposed to get home and take Matt to soccer, but I got tied up at the office. She called, and I told her that I couldn't get there and that she could take him, knowing full well that the only way to get him there on time was I-35 in rush-hour traffic. She left Kenzie with a neighbor and…" His eyes stung and he couldn't even say the words.

Hanna pulled the sheet fully around them both. "You had no way of knowing." She kissed his cheek and hugged him tight. "Things happen. Nobody could blame you."

Except himself and he knew he was at fault. He could have taken the work home and done it after soccer. He could have done it the next day. He could have told Belinda that it was just practice and to blow it off. "Instead of belittling her fear, I should have taught her to drive on freeways and in traffic. Then they'd both be alive."

He felt tears against his bare shoulder, and Hanna rubbed her cheek. "It's time to forgive yourself. Don't beat yourself up over hindsight." Through his blurry vision, her liquid brown eyes stared into his. She blotted the corner of his eye with the sheet. "You are a good guy and a loving father. You never intended anyone any harm."

Rubbing Hanna's back, Vince buried his face in her soft hair and felt his body tremble. "I didn't protect my family.

For whatever reason, God left me one last chance. To be a good father to Kenzie. That won't make it up to Belinda, but it's something."

As Hanna held him and let him cry, he realized he'd never felt as close to another human being. At least not in nine years. But facing his own vulnerability scared the shit out of him. "I've gotta get outta here."

He lifted her away and yanked his T-shirt over his head. Shoving his feet into his cowboy boots, all he could think of was getting out of that room before he broke down completely and made a bigger fool of himself.

"Vince, wait!"

But he couldn't face her, not right now.

Chapter Twelve

Hanna's heart shattered for Vince. Would he ever not blame himself? It finally registered why he was so insistent on teaching Kenzie to take care of herself. It was his way of protecting her. Of making sure that what happened to her mother didn't happen to her.

Hanna crawled off the bed and wandered to the balcony doors. Could she help him? Could anyone heal that hurt? At loose ends, she showered and dressed, straightened the room. The drizzle had subsided into a fog as she stepped out onto the balcony for the third time to see if Vince was walking the river. The water taxis glided by on their endless loop, but no sign of Vince. She wanted to give him space to deal with his emotions, yet she wanted him to come back. She needed to hold him.

She considered going down to the lobby, but wanted to make sure she was here when he returned. She picked up her camera and scrolled through the pictures from the day before. He appeared so happy and carefree on the surface. But it just proved you never really knew someone. He'd been living with this guilt for nine years. How could anyone get over losing a spouse and child?

Laying the camera on the table, she thumbed through the entertainment rag, but not even the insane headlines warranted a smile.

The room door clicked quietly shut. She turned from the balcony and her gaze met Vince's. His navy T-shirt was damp and stuck to his chest. His hair curled over his forehead from the humidity.

Holding back from rushing to wrap him in her arms, she slowly walked toward him. "You okay?"

"Yeah." Shrugging, he stuffed his hands in his pockets. "Chilled."

"Hop in the shower and I'll make another pot of coffee."

"Thanks." He dug dry clothes out of his bag and headed into the bathroom. By the time he padded barefoot out of the steamy bathroom, dressed in jeans and a gray plaid flannel, she handed him a fresh cup of coffee.

Curling his long fingers around the cup, he took a sip. "I'm sorry for unloading on you."

She poured herself a cup and tried to find the right words for what she wanted to say. "My divorce pales in comparison to what you went through. But we all live with regrets. We all have things we wish we'd done differently if only we'd known."

"Richard screwed around on you. Not sure how that translates into you being the guilty party."

"Men aren't the only ones who get caught up in their roles and responsibilities in a relationship. I should have put more energy into my marriage and not put it all into Ashton, the house, charities, all those things that I thought equated to a perfect life. Then maybe my husband wouldn't have needed another woman."

"That's crap. If a guy wants to screw around, he does. He may blame the wife, but most likely that's just because he feels guilty and has to transfer it to someone rather than himself."

She grinned. "I can't believe you said that. I mean, it's so obvious to women that men don't handle guilt well, but I had no idea that you realized it."

"Oh, we realize it. We just don't typically admit it." He winked. "You caught me on an uncharacteristically vulnerable day."

"Men." Hanna grinned. "See, I had a dream too, Vince. Richard and I had a beautiful home and two expensive cars. Ashton was in private school. We had tons of friends. Membership in the country club. I thought we had the life we both dreamed of. The life I left Marble Falls for, you know? Like you, I wanted something different than what I grew up with."

"Did he give you an excuse as to why he started running around?"

"Said he'd fallen in love with someone else who fulfilled him as a man. Failed to mention that she was a twenty-three-year-old law student interning in his office and the daughter of one of the firm's founders."

Vince leaned forward and touched her face. "So returning home to Marble Falls signifies the end of your fantasy? Not just the failed marriage, but all those things you'd dreamed about and obtained before he yanked it all out from under you?"

"Pretty much. But at least I got to live it for thirteen years. And now I'm going to make this bookstore work and start over. It's never too late. When I was a little girl Mom always bought me books or took me to the library. We both loved to escape into a good book. She and I would talk about opening our own bookstore, but she knew my dream didn't involve spending my life in Marble Falls. She wanted me to be happy. Like you said, dreams change." She sniffed. "Vince, you should finish your Masters. Take Mackenzie and work abroad. It'd be a fantastic experience for both of you."

He rolled the coffee cup between his hands. "I'm finally

content with my life. Kenzie is a kick. My in-laws are supportive and all-around good folks. They give her all the love and family she lost when Belinda and Matt died. My parents are an hour away and spoil her rotten. My business is successful. Life is good." He winked. "Your purse is vibrating."

"Oh, crap! I put my phone on vibrate yesterday after Tiffany called." She jumped up and dug her phone out of her purse. "Hello."

"Where the hell are you?" Richard barked. "You didn't answer your phone all damn night. Your mother wouldn't tell me a thing."

A million horrible thoughts filled Hanna's mind. "Richard, what's wrong? Why have you been calling me all night?"

"We spent the night in the emergency room. The pain medication they prescribed for Ashton reacted with his asthma meds and he couldn't breathe. You didn't tell me he was allergic to pain meds."

Oh, God. She knew something like this was bound to happen. "Is he okay?"

"They put him on oxygen." Richard didn't elaborate further.

"But how is he right now? I can be there in a few hours."

"He's home and resting, Hanna. It was last night that you could've shed some light on what we should do." Richard sounded like a petulant child.

All Hanna could think about was getting to Ashton, making sure he was okay. "I'll be there as soon as I can."

"No. This is my week with him. You and the cowboy enjoy whatever it is you're doing. Phoebe and I handled things." The connection clicked off in her ear.

She stared at the phone and tried to get a grip. Richard knew she was with Vince? Was Ashton really okay? And even if he wasn't, unless Richard wanted her there, she had no right. Her baby had been struggling to breathe and had

had to rely on a woman he hardly knew and a father who'd seldom had to deal with his asthma. Hanna had always been the one to watch out for him and nurse him through.

Vince touched her shoulder. "What's wrong?"

Turning to him, she was stunned that he was even in the room. "I have no business being here with you. What kind of mother doesn't hear her phone when her son is in the emergency room?" She darted around the suite, gathering the rest of her belongings. Stuffing her new sundress and shoes into the bag, she spotted her bra from the night before under the edge of the bed. As she stooped to retrieve it, Vince grabbed her arm.

"Slow down. Is Ashton okay?"

"He's fine now, but he wasn't last night and they couldn't reach me."

Vince leaned down and looked into her eyes. "Okay, but he's out of danger now. You're overreacting a little, don't you think?"

"I'd have never forgiven myself if Ashton hadn't made it because I turned my phone down so it wouldn't interrupt my romantic getaway. What kind of self-absorbed mother does that? We can't just decide not to have responsibilities. Who am I kidding? We have responsibilities, Vince. We're parents 24/7 whether the kids are actually with us or not." She jerked away, stomped into the bathroom and stuffed her cosmetics and toothbrush into her bag.

When she came out, he grasped both her shoulders. "Nobody said we weren't responsible parents. We're entitled to a break. That doesn't make you a bad mother or me a bad father."

She felt like a bad mother. Ashton was the one thing that she'd done right and even that was going down the tubes since the divorce. He was always angry at her. Thought she was screwing up his life. But the one thing he'd never complained about was her being there to help when he couldn't breathe, and now she'd even failed at that. Zipping the case shut, she tried to calm down enough so Vince didn't think she was a raving lunatic.

Shouldering her purse, she turned to him. "Vince, this was a mistake. I can't pretend to be someone I'm not."

He shoved his hands into his pockets and didn't say a word, didn't try to stop her.

By the time she got to her car, she was crying and shaking so hard she couldn't drive. She tossed her bag in and leaned her head against the steering wheel. There wasn't one single thing in her life that she hadn't messed up.

Hanna sat in the car until she'd calmed down enough to drive. She had so many thoughts bouncing around in her mind, she probably shouldn't have been behind the wheel at all, but she couldn't sit here in this parking lot.

Just outside of Marble Falls, she stopped for gas and made a side trip to the ladies' room. She washed her face and dried it with a paper towel, then brushed on a touch of blush, eye shadow and lip gloss. Mom already didn't approve of this little getaway. The last thing she needed was for Norma to realize she'd been crying.

Feeling slightly refreshed, she drove the last few miles into town and parked across the street from Bluebonnet Books. She found her mother checking out one lone customer, a man buying three books.

"Did Richard get hold of you last night?" The cash register rang as Norma closed the drawer.

"I talked to him this morning. Ashton's okay." Hanna blew out a breath and smiled as the gentleman, with a camera around his neck and his new map of the Hill Country in hand, closed the door behind him. "Sorry to put you on the spot with Richard last night, Mom."

Mom shrugged. "It happens. It just upset me that Ashton

was sick and we couldn't reach you. I'd have called your hotel, but I didn't know where you were staying."

"It was my fault for putting my phone on vibrate. I meant to turn the ringer back on, but I forgot."

"I guess Vince can be rather distracting."

That was an understatement. Hanna's emotions surrounding Vince were too raw to verbalize, especially with her mother. "Everything run okay here?"

Norma narrowed one eye as if weighing the wisdom of pushing the point. "We've been busy with the lunch-hour rush. Anne Haythorn stopped in and helped out for a bit. She said she was sorry to miss you. But that woman keeps close tabs on every move Vince makes. I'm sure she was just fishing to see if you and Vince were out of town together."

"Mom! Don't start." Hanna gritted her teeth and headed for the minuscule office to put away her purse.

Norma leaned against the doorjamb and sighed. "Sweetie, I just don't want you to rush into something too soon. Your pride has been bruised, and I'm afraid you're on the rebound and are going to be hurt again."

Hanna knew her mother's concern was genuine, yet she also knew she would keep questioning until she knew every detail. "I know, Mom. If it makes you feel any better, I ended it. It's too soon for me to consider a relationship."

Mom poured two cups of coffee. "I think that's wise."

Taking one of the cups, Hanna knew she'd made the right choice by breaking things off. "San Antonio was lovely though."

Norma shivered. "With all that humidity?"

Here she went again with her dislike of San Antonio. "Has to be more than humidity to turn you against such a beautiful, romantic city. Have you ever been?"

Norma gripped her cup. "Once. A long time ago."

"With Daddy?"

"No, not with your father." Norma gulped down half her coffee. "It was nothing. A long time ago. Way before you were born."

"Another guy?" Hanna wasn't sure how much she really wanted to know. Her mother talked about everyone else, but seldom about herself. Especially not about the past.

"I may need something stronger than this if we're going to talk about all that."

Hanna's stomach knotted. "Did you love Daddy?"

"Yes, I loved your father." Mom pushed the cup back. "But he wasn't the love of my life. The man I went to San Antonio with, the man I first gave my heart to, died in Vietnam. After that I never had the desire to return to San Antonio."

"You didn't know Daddy then?"

"I knew him. After Brad was killed, your dad started calling me. They were friends and I think Daddy wanted us to help each other grieve for Brad. It took him two years to convince me to marry him, but I finally gave in. Not the life I'd envisioned, but I've never regretted it. Your daddy gave me a good life, probably better than what I had planned." Norma smiled. "And he gave me you."

Hanna's eyes filled with tears, and she stood up and wrapped her arms around her mom. "Thanks for that. I guess that's just the way life goes. Best-laid plans…"

Norma patted Hanna's back. "I'm going to enjoy having you close by to share things with."

Maybe her mother was finally starting to see her as an adult. "It's nice to be close again. Get to know each other as women."

Pulling back, Mom laughed. "Yes, it is. But you'll always be my little girl."

Hanna's heart warmed. Just like Ashton would always be her beautiful baby boy. "I know."

"So, it didn't work out well with Vince?"

Not an easy question to answer, but her mom had shared an extremely personal experience. "It worked out too well. It scares me how easily Vince drew me in. I don't think I realized how vulnerable I am right now. My emotions are all over the place. The last thing I need is to rush into a possible second mistake while I'm still raw from Richard."

"Richard is a good father." Mom shrugged. "No matter what happened between the two of you, he loves Ashton."

"Yes, he does. But Vince is giving Ashton self-confidence, guy confidence. I know I can't do that, and Richard doesn't even realize Ashton doesn't have it."

"So you're interested in Vince for what he does for Ashton's self-esteem?"

Hanna closed her eyes and thought back to the attentive lover and sexy body she'd just spent twenty-four hours with. It would be so easy if Vince's attentiveness to Ashton was all there was. "Getting to know Vince was an extremely pleasant surprise. He's not at all what I expected when I met him. But it'd be awkward, unfair to ask him to continue to mentor Ashton since I told him I couldn't keep seeing him."

"Ashton will be okay."

Maybe, but Hanna knew how important Vince and Mackenzie had become in Ashton's life. And now she'd cost him his new hero. It was just one more thing her angry preteen would hold against her.

Chapter Thirteen

Hanna idled the engine and squinted to focus through the rain-streaked windshield. She didn't want to miss Ashton when he came out of school. The spring storm had rolled in a couple of hours ago, and she didn't trust him not to get on the back of Kenzie's bike and head home on the slick streets. Good judgment had not been in abundance of late where her son was concerned.

Or herself.

She caught sight of Ashton and Kenzie as they raced from the bike rack, pushing the electric bicycle. By the time Hanna jumped out to wave them down, they were already down the sidewalk and Vince was loading the bike into the bed of his pickup. The kids piled into the cab, and Hanna crawled back into her car, unseen. At least they weren't on that bike in this weather.

What a madhouse. Shaking the rain off her arms, she cranked up the defrost and looked for a break in the bumper-to-bumper SUVs. Parents and kids dashed through the downpour in between cars. Just as Hanna spotted a gap in the line of cars, her cell phone chimed.

She put the car back in Park and fished the phone out of her purse. "Mackenzie?"

"Hey, Mom, it's Ashton. I'll be at Kenzie's. Vince is going to do his paperwork while we're doing homework. Then he said if we were done early enough and it was okay with you, he'd spring for pizza before he brings me home."

"Ashton, you don't want to impose on Mr. Keegan." Since she'd decided not to see Vince anymore, she wasn't sure about him continuing to be such a big part of Ashton's daily activities. Ashton was attached enough as it was.

"Please, Mom. He offered. I didn't ask."

"Please!" Kenzie pleaded in the background.

Hanna didn't have the heart to say no. This was the first day back in school after spring break and they probably wanted to catch up. "Okay, but tell Vince to let me know if it'd make it easier if I picked you up. I do not want us putting him out."

VINCE FOLLOWED THE KIDS into the house and grinned as Boo's tail started wagging. The silly dog was getting as attached to Ashton as he was to Kenzie. "Kenzie, go get on dry clothes. And toss Ashton that navy-blue sweatsuit. It should fit well enough while I dry his clothes."

While the kids were getting dry, Vince changed his shirt and jeans. That rain was chilly. He put on a pot of coffee and heated milk for hot chocolate for the kids. They could all use a warm-up.

"Put your wet clothes in the dryer." He nodded toward the laundry room, then tossed Boo a biscuit.

Kenzie started the dryer and came back out. "Summer softball signup is tomorrow."

"I know." Kenzie had been playing every summer since she was five.

She dug a bag of cookies out of the pantry and grinned at Ashton. "So you're still not going to sign up?"

"Nobody would want me on their team." Ashton took a cookie in one hand and rubbed Boo with the other.

"So who cares? Sign up anyway."

"Nah, I don't think so. Everybody else has been playing for years and I'm still learning."

Vince set the two cups of hot chocolate on the bar in front of them. "Do you want to play?"

Ashton shrugged. "I'm not good enough. The guys would make fun of me."

"Can't succeed if you don't put yourself out there." Vince poured himself a cup of coffee. He'd never met a kid with such low self-confidence, especially when it came to sports.

"Mom probably wouldn't let me anyway with my asthma. And I'd have to change the weeks I'm at Dad's."

"If you want to play, my dad can talk to your mom," Kenzie volunteered.

"Ashton can ask his mom," Vince said. After San Antonio, he wasn't about to challenge Hanna on how to raise her son again. "You've come a long way on your batting, Ashton. Kenzie and I practice almost every night during the season. You're welcome to come over and join us."

"You think I could get good enough?"

Vince took a sip of coffee. "The only sure way to fail is—"

"To not even try." Kenzie finished the sentence for him. "He says that a lot," she explained to Ashton.

"Okay, busted." Vince laughed. "Now jump on that homework and let me get a couple of bids out. My stomach's growling, and I can already taste that pizza. Are we going to order in or go out?"

"Order in so I have time to beat Ash on Wii NASCAR."

"In your dreams," Ashton said, opening his backpack.

A loud clap of thunder vibrated the windows, and Vince decided staying in was definitely the best plan. "Give it your best shots. I'll take down the winner."

"Not!" Kenzie laughed.

Vince went into his office and booted up the laptop, but

he could hear the kids talking and laughing. Kenzie was not going to let Ashton off the hook on the baseball deal. She had plenty of friends, but he'd never known her to take to a kid quite like she had to Ashton. It was strange because she typically didn't have much patience with kids who weren't like her. Even when they weren't together, she was talking about some funny thing Ashton said or did.

Vince minimized the spreadsheet he was working on and opened his picture folder. Hanna on the Guadalupe River. Hanna and the kids in the field of bluebonnets. Hanna and him on the river taxi in San Antonio. Hell, it wasn't just his daughter who had an obsession with the Rossers.

Hanna's decision to work through her post-divorce issues and figure out where her life was going made perfect, rational sense. The flawless rhythm of her body in unison with his had just as much merit. How could something that felt that right be wrong? What they'd shared on that trip had been too intense, physically and emotionally, not to give it a chance.

She owed it to herself to get her head straight before jumping into another relationship—he'd never deny her that. But there was a niggling fear that maybe he'd frightened her by coming clean about his past with Belinda. It sure as hell had frightened him. God, he'd never gone into that crap with anyone else, and it was way too early in the relationship to have gone there with Hanna. She likely thought he was a total jackass.

Probably because his brain was still in a San Antonio hotel room, the kids finished their assignments before he was done with his proposal. They plugged in the Wii and he was serenaded with the sounds of race cars and cheering as they got into the competition.

"If you'd just use your instincts and play instead of analyzing how the game works, you might actually win." Evidently Kenzie had won the first race.

"Games are really pretty simple," Ashton explained. "It's just a program that reacts to how you move."

"Yeah, yeah, yeah. Next race. Quit thinking and drive, Ash! I've almost got a full lap on you."

It was almost eight by the time they finished their pizza and Vince drove Ashton home. Hanna opened the door when they pulled up and Vince got out. He hadn't actually seen her since she'd run out of the hotel room.

Her hair was kinky from the humidity and she looked comfortable in a pair of faded jeans and a huge white blouse. No makeup. No jewelry. No logical reason his libido was kicking up, but he couldn't stop staring at her. In his defense, she didn't break eye contact, either.

"Mom, here's a paper on softball sign-ups tomorrow."

She blinked her beautiful dark eyes, and took the paper from Ashton. "Oh, honey, I don't know about all that running with your asthma."

"I want to do it. Vince said the only way I can fail is by not trying at all. And I can practice every day with him and Kenzie. I'm getting better."

Here it came again. She was going to jump down his throat about encouraging Ashton. She glanced back at Vince. "Ashton, go take your shower. Let me talk to Vince a minute."

Oh, yeah. This wasn't going to be pretty.

Ashton went inside, but turned. "Thanks for the pizza. Kenzie said you'd have to talk to her."

Now he was getting "I told you so" from the kid? "You're welcome, Ashton."

Hanna stepped out on the covered porch with Vince and closed the door. The rain dripped off the roof and splattered in a puddle behind the bushes. "Softball and asthma aren't a good mix."

"It's important to him. How about if I promise to be at all his games to keep an eye on him?"

"Vince, I'm not sure what to say here. You aren't obligated to look out for Ashton."

He tilted his head. "I'm not doing it under any obligation. He's a good kid and my daughter's friend and, no offense, but he needs a guy around."

She took a deep breath and reached one hand out and let the next drop of rain land on her palm, then turned her hand to let it drip off. Anything to avoid looking at him probably. "Yes, but how can we handle this after..."

Shoving his hands in his pockets so he didn't touch her, he leaned around and captured her gaze. "We're friends. That hasn't changed. We have kids to raise. It's a small town. I don't want us to feel uncomfortable around each other every time we're together. Truce?"

The corners of her mouth turned up. "We can try."

"What happened in those two days was pretty cool. Too cool to let it ruin a good friendship."

"It was more than cool." She smiled, but nibbled her lip. "And I do value your friendship."

He winked. "I'll try not to picture you naked if you'll try not to picture me naked. Deal?"

"Oh, that helps keep things casual." She laughed. "It was childish of me to run away like that. I'm sorry."

"And softball?"

"Let me think about that one."

HANNA FINALLY GAVE IN and signed Ashton up for softball. He assured her that he was going to give it his all and that he'd use his inhaler anytime he needed it no matter who was watching. What convinced her was that he admitted he knew he might fail, but he wanted to take the risk. How could she deny him that chance when he was just beginning to fit in?

On Thursday, when the kids arrived at the bookstore, Kenzie went straight to the bathroom. Ashton dropped his backpack in one of the chairs by the coffee center. "Is it okay if Kenzie stays here and we do homework together? Then when Vince gets off, we're going to her house to toss a few balls."

"Sure. Offer her a cookie and a soft drink when she comes out." She hugged his shoulders. "Just keep the noise level down."

By the time Hanna had helped a couple of regular customers pick out some of the latest romance novels, Kenzie still hadn't returned from the bathroom.

Hanna checked the ladies out at the register and put their books into a bag. Ashton was working away on his homework. Something was up or Kenzie would be out by now. As soon as the women left, Hanna walked to the back of the shop and knocked on the restroom door. "Kenzie, are you okay?"

Nothing. Not a sound.

"Kenzie?"

Finally a very weak "Yeah" came from inside.

"Are you sick?"

"Not exactly. My stomach hurts way down low."

Hanna nibbled her lip. Twelve years old. Stomach cramps. Oh, dear. "Are you bleeding?"

"Yes. I'm not sure what to do."

"Hold on. Let me get you something."

Hanna went to her office, pulled a sanitary pad from her purse and returned to the bathroom. "Open the door."

Slowly it opened, and Kenzie looked up at her. Her face was pale and she'd been crying.

Hanna handed her the pad. "Everything's fine. Take your time and I'll drive you home. Okay?"

Kenzie nodded and closed the door.

Hanna filled her mother in and told Ashton that Kenzie

wasn't feeling well. She gathered up Kenzie's backpack and asked Ashton to put her bike in the office until Vince could come by and pick it up. Then she called Vince and told him what was happening.

His voice sounded shaky. "Is she okay? Do I need to come get her?"

"No, I'll get her home. You might want to stop and grab a few supplies. Do you know what to buy?" Hanna figured the way Kenzie looked, she shouldn't put her through stopping by the store on the way home.

There was total quiet for a few seconds. Vince at a loss for words: that was one thing she'd never expected. "Maybe I should meet you at the house and you can make me a list."

"Okay." Hanna wasn't sure whether he just needed to see his daughter and make sure she was being taken care of or whether he was in shock. "She'll get through this, Vince. We all do."

Hanna led Mackenzie to the car and placed the backpack on the backseat. "You feeling any better? Maybe an aspirin would help."

She shrugged. "I don't think so. I'm not sure what 'better' is supposed to feel like."

Mackenzie crawled into the car and buckled her seat belt, but leaned against the window as if the cool glass helped.

Hanna drove the short distance to the house, and Mackenzie darted into the bathroom and closed the door.

The shower started and Hanna heard the pickup door slam. Vince bolted into the kitchen. "Is she scared?"

On impulse she gave him a hug. "A little. Want me to run to the drugstore?"

He glanced down the hall at the closed bathroom door. "Maybe you should stay here and just make me that list."

Wow, he really *was* feeling out of his comfort zone. Hanna quickly jotted down a few items. "You could also pick up some ginger ale and whatever kind of soup or comfort food she likes. She might be queasy tonight."

"You sure you're okay here?"

"I'm fine. Mackenzie will be fine." She pushed him toward the door.

Hanna dug through her purse and pulled out another pad. She knocked on the bathroom door. "Kenzie, I'm leaving this right here by the door. I'm here if you need me."

The shower stopped. "Thanks." Hanna moved away from the door, but Mackenzie stuck her head out. "Where's my dad?"

"He ran to the store to get what you need."

"Does he know what happened?"

Hanna grinned. "Of course he knows. He was married to your mom for years. I'm sure this isn't the first time he's had to make an emergency run. Can I get you a nightgown?"

Mackenzie nodded. "Second drawer on the right. I'd like the blue one with the butterflies."

So far so good. Surprisingly the room was neat and organized. The walls were bright yellow and the spread sported a white daisy pattern. Hanna located the gown and fresh panties easily enough. She handed the items through the crack in the door and went to the kitchen for a glass of water. By the time she returned with a daisy-painted glass of ice water, Mackenzie was snuggled under the covers, her knees drawn up to her tummy. She looked so young to be going through this. Her face was pale and her blond hair spread across the pillow, still damp from the shower.

Hmmm, how to approach her. "Feel better?"

Mackenzie nodded.

At least she wasn't belligerent about Hanna being here. "I'm not sure what to say. Do you have any questions?"

The girl actually met her eyes. "The nurse talked to us and

gave us all a pamphlet in health class. And I can ask Dad or Grandma."

"Okay. But if you think of something, I'd be happy to try to answer. You hungry?"

Kenzie puffed out her cheeks. "My stomach hurts bad enough already."

"Try to relax. That always helps me. I'll be in the kitchen."

Hanna actually felt sorry for Kenzie, although she didn't seem like the same feisty girl who typically kept things stirred up.

Hanna's stomach growled, and she figured Vince would be hungry, too, since it was almost dinnertime. She rummaged in the fridge and made a turkey-and-cheese sandwich. She grinned. Even the plates had a daisy pattern that matched the canister set.

Gravel crunched as the pickup pulled in. She grabbed a soda out of the fridge and placed it on the bar beside the sandwich.

When Vince walked through the door, he put the bag on the counter and looked around. "Everything okay?"

"She's resting. The thought of food makes her nauseous and she doesn't want to discuss it."

He pulled the Midol out. "You think this would help?"

"You could call her doctor and ask, but I don't see that half a tablet could hurt."

"Me, either." He took out a knife and split one tablet. "I'll go check on her."

The door was open and Hanna could hear the conversation almost as if they were in the room with her.

"Hey, punkin', how you feeling?"

"Like crap."

Leave it to Mackenzie to put things into perspective.

"Here, see if this helps."

The bed springs squeaked and Hanna heard a slurp of water. "So, are you okay, Dad?"

Short pause. "No, but we'll get through this like we have everything else. It's just nature."

"Nature sucks green pond scum."

He laughed. "You rest. Hanna and I'll be in the kitchen. Yell if you need anything."

"Can you turn on my new CD? Then maybe I can whip you at NASCAR later."

"In your dreams. Ain't gonna happen in this lifetime."

Rascal Flats filtered through the air and the bedroom door clicked shut. Vince walked back into the kitchen. "Isn't she sort of young for this? I thought I'd ask my mother-in-law to talk to her this summer, but I figured that might even be rushing things. Geesh. She's barely twelve."

Hanna watched as he paced the room. Instinctively she reached out and wrapped her arms around his waist. She'd never seen anyone who looked more like they needed a hug. Her body trembled the instant it touched his. San Antonio. River taxis. Intimate hotel rooms and rainstorms. She felt his heart rate accelerate as if they were sharing the same wavelength.

She pulled back before she gave in to the temptation to kiss him. "Next we'll see how you handle Mackenzie dating."

"Yeah, let's not talk about that right now."

All Hanna could think about was how homey and intimate the little kitchen felt. How she should not be nearly as sexually aware of the man in front of her as she was. She needed to get out of here.

She nodded toward the bar. "I made you a sandwich."

"I appreciate all you've done today."

What was she supposed to do with her hands? "Not half as much as you do for Ashton."

That blue stare bored into her and held her captive.

"I need to go."

"Don't." Before she could take a step, his hand reached out and he pulled her to him. His lips touched hers, demanding and receiving. His tongue exploring and enticing.

Pressing her body into his embrace, she rubbed her hands up his back and tangled them around his neck. The short hair at the nape of his neck tickled her fingertips, but she could do little more than groan in satisfaction at the familiar scent of shampoo and sweat.

"Hanna," he whispered against her lips as he cupped her butt and held her tight against him. "I don't want to be your friend."

Chapter Fourteen

That evening Hanna scrolled through the pictures from both the tubing trip and the San Antonio trip, as she'd gotten in the habit of doing before bedtime.

Her body still tingled with sensation from Vince's touch, his kisses. Who was she kidding? Vince was right. She didn't want to be friends either, at least not "just" friends. She shut down the laptop and crawled into bed, imagining Vince's hands on her body and his mouth on hers.

She snuggled under the covers and closed her eyes, but her mind was too awake to sleep. Could they make this relation-ship work? It was too soon. And she was taking a huge risk. And it might not work out. And...her cell phone chimed.

She glanced at the display and grinned. "Hey."

"Hey," Vince said. "Kenzie's finally asleep."

"She having a hard time?"

"She's miserable. Stomach hurts, back hurts, head hurts and she's irritable as a hornet. I called her doctor, and she said to give her a full tablet every four hours if she needed it. She also wants to see her next week."

"That's probably a good idea."

The guy sounded exhausted.

"She decided she'd rather suck on a Popsicle than eat her Grandma's vegetable soup. And it's her favorite."

"So are you going to keep her home tomorrow?"

"Unless she does a major turnaround, I don't see her going to school. Maybe she'll at least feel like doing her homework. My mother-in-law is going to pick up her assignments, and Kenzie will probably go home with her for the day."

"Next month will be easier, I bet."

She heard the bed springs creak. "I sure as hell hope so. If this is what I'm in for every month, I'm clueless. She never falls apart."

Poor guy. He'd dealt with diapers, being a single parent, school and probably all the childhood illnesses, but this was more than he'd bargained for.

"Ashton asked what was wrong with Mackenzie," she said. "I guess I pulled the same trick you did. Couldn't figure out the right words. I'm stuttering, and he says, 'So, is it that girl cycle thing?'"

"And you just answered yes?"

"Yep." Hanna grinned at how well they could read each other. It was nice to have another parent who understood kids and wasn't afraid to admit when he didn't have all the answers. God, she'd just like to hold him. Sleep in his arms. "Vince."

"Yeah?"

"I…I miss you tonight." If she wasn't careful, she could fall in love with this man.

"I miss you, too. We'll make this work. Sweet dreams."

BLUEBONNET BOOKS was getting busier each day, which was a good thing. With any luck, it was more than the novelty of a new shop in town and everyone would continue to stop by. Even if each patron only purchased one item, it could add up.

Hanna was getting ready to lock up when the front-door bell jingled. "Mrs. Maguire. Nice to see you. How is Kenzie today?"

"Much better this afternoon. Her father got home early."

There was a slight hesitation, but she nodded. "We do appreciate your helping out yesterday, but don't worry about Kenzie. We can take care of her."

We? As in "the family"? "I was glad I could be there for Kenzie and Vince."

"Vince has handled things for the past nine years better than most men would've. He did sound a little out of his element when he called me last night."

The woman's tone was friendly enough, but her message came across crystal-clear. *You're not family. Vince called me.* The last thing Hanna intended was to threaten Vince's ex-mother-in-law's role in his and Kenzie's lives, but obviously her handling of the situation had done just that.

"I'm glad to hear that Mackenzie is better. Can I help you with anything?"

"Kenzie likes adventure books."

Hanna showed her to the children's section and the appropriate shelf. "Just sing out if you have any questions."

"Are you sure this is smart?" Hanna asked as Vince closed the garage door at his house and helped her out of the truck.

"Not sure about smart." He backed her against the truck and covered her mouth with his. "But you gotta admit it sure feels right."

That it did. "And you don't think Mrs. Haythorn will notice me walking into your house with you at 6:00 p.m.? People are getting home from work now."

He laughed and pulled her close against his side. "Keep your head down until we get inside the house. Even if she does spot us, she won't know who you are. It'll give her something new to ponder."

Hanna followed him across the lawn and tried to figure out just how much of this they could possibly hope to keep from burning up the phone lines. "And she'll call my mom to ponder it with her. 'Oh my, who is Vince Keegan sleeping with now? Is it Donna Martin's daughter, Kim? Or perhaps some new victim?'"

"Kim? How the hell do you know about Kim? Oh yeah, you live with the town gossip. What other interesting incidents of impropriety have I had?"

Hanna bumped him with her hip. "They must not have been that interesting if you don't even remember. But I'll see what I can dig up for you when I get home."

He flashed those deep dimples. "Just want to make sure I didn't miss anything good."

"Mrs. Haythorn will be positively gleeful when she discovers it's me sleeping with you. My mom told the ladies at church about Mrs. Haythorn's daughter having a bun in the oven and having to get married."

"Seriously? A bun in the oven?" He dropped his bag on the chair and checked the messages on his machine. A couple from Gray and an invitation to dinner Sunday at "the folks."

Why did it make her uneasy to think about how much a part of the Maguire family Vince remained after nine years?

Hanna wasn't ready to expose their new relationship by having a dinner out, so Vince pulled bacon and eggs out of the fridge.

"The man is good in bed *and* he cooks."

He placed the bacon in the skillet and then bowed. "Thank you, on both counts. My mother-in-law is not a fan of McDonald's and was afraid Kenzie might become malnourished. She had us over almost every night and finally took it upon herself to teach me to cook. I make a mean beef stew with all fresh vegetables and corn bread that can warm you up on a cold night. I suck at pies, though."

Hanna was torn between admiring Vince for remaining so close to Belinda's family and letting it make her uncomfortable.

How would they react when the news hit town that he had a new girlfriend?

They hadn't even gotten dinner cooked when someone knocked on the back door. Vince set the plate of bacon on the table and opened the door. Boo bounded inside, tail wagging and tongue lolling out as Vince bent and scratched him behind the ears.

Grayson Maguire followed the dog into the room. Not quite as tall as Vince, but similar style of dress. Tight, faded jeans, work boots and a ball cap, only his cap and dark-green button-down sported a Maguire Landscaping logo. "I had a job in town and thought I'd drop him off. Since Kenzie was in the house instead of playing with him, Boo decided to dig up the flowers Mom just planted." He eyed Hanna and shuffled from one foot to the other.

"Great, guess I get the opportunity to replant, courtesy of Boo?"

Gray rubbed the dog's head as Boo ambled back his way. "No permanent damage."

Vince glanced from Grayson to Hanna. "Oh, do you know Hanna Rosser? Hanna, Grayson Maguire, my brother-in-law and salvation when I need a day or two's break from work. We trade out."

Gray removed his cap and extended his hand. "Hi, Hanna. Nice to see you back in town." Dark, straight hair and nervous gray eyes that seemed to want to look anywhere rather than at her.

"It's been a long time." She shook his hand. He obviously wasn't comfortable with her being here, but she didn't know what else to do except be friendly.

"Years. Not since graduation." Glancing around the kitchen, he backed toward the door. "Well, don't let me interrupt your dinner. I need to get back over to the folks."

"Tell Mom thanks for keeping Kenzie." Vince shook his

head as Gray tugged his cap back on and practically bolted out the door. "Can't say that I've seen him that nervous since some hot little redhead came on to him one night at dinner."

"He was always quiet. Not as outgoing as his three older brothers."

"Yep, still is."

"I don't think Grayson was thrilled with finding me here."

Vince cracked eggs into the sizzling skillet and tossed the shells in the garbage. "Nah, don't take it personally. Gray's just got trust issues when it comes to contemporary women."

Hanna grinned, opening drawers until she located the silverware. "Wants a woman like his mom? Stay-at-home wife, dinner-on-the-table-at-six sort of woman?"

"Claire Maguire is a hard act to follow." Vince scooped the scrambled eggs into a bowl and grabbed the toast out of the toaster.

"I'm sure." She placed napkins and silverware on the table. Claire and Wayne Maguire were the grassroots of the community. Steadfast, good, upstanding citizens. Even Hanna's mother was hesitant to gossip about any of the Maguire brood.

Claire was everything Hanna no longer had the luxury of being. Hanna didn't have a husband to take care of her and pay the bills so that she could stay home and take care of Ashton and the house. Another adjustment to her new status in life.

AFTER DINNER, THE DOG stretched out on his back on the rug in front of the cold fireplace, all four paws in the air. Hanna and Vince settled in on the sofa to watch a movie, but she couldn't help worrying that the neighbors somehow knew she was here. Vince's answer to that was to wait until the lights were out in every house before taking her home. That might have worked, except her mother and Ashton would be home from dinner and the movie in a couple of hours. "I have to be home by ten or I turn into a pumpkin, so…"

Boo's ears perked up and he rolled to his feet at the sound of a second knock at the back door. Hanna narrowed her eyes at Vince. "Doesn't anyone come to the front door around here?"

With a sigh, he stood, straightened his shirt and headed into the kitchen. "Salesmen, sometimes."

Hanna recognized Mrs. Haythorn's Southern drawl and stayed discreetly out of sight in the living room.

"I saw Kenzie leave with Claire this afternoon. Just noticed your lights on. Thought you might like a piece of homemade apple pie."

"Appreciate it," Vince said. "But you didn't have to do that."

"Figured you might be hungry. I mowed your side yard. Out mowing mine anyway this morning before it got hot."

"You're a sweetheart, but you don't need to mow my lawn, Mrs. Haythorn."

"No problem at all. Ran out of gas or I'd have gotten the front, too. My granddaughter is spending the day tomorrow. Thought I'd see if Kenzie wanted to come over and bake cookies."

"She's spending the day at her grandmother's. She'll be sorry she missed seeing Molly."

"Molly will be disappointed. Was that Grayson Maguire dropping off Boo earlier?"

"That was Gray."

"Sweet man. He needs a good wife, too."

"Gray will figure it out. You take care now, okay?"

The back door shut and the deadbolt clicked into place before Hanna let out her breath.

Vince padded barefoot back into the room. "That woman needs a life."

Boo flopped back down on his rug as if disgruntled with the interruption of his nap.

Hanna rubbed her forehead. "Wow, she's persistent. She knew someone was here, you know?"

"Yeah, kept trying to lean around me to see who was in here."

"So is Molly Mrs. Haythorn's granddaughter?" Hanna tried to piece together the lives of the townsfolk since she'd been gone.

"Yeah, thirteen-year-old Molly, not to be confused with her eighteen-year-old sister, Candace, who I recently learned from you was already in the oven when her scandalous parents married. I was shocked!"

"Oh yeah, because we know that never happens." Hanna giggled, but it really wasn't funny. Her mother's little network of friends would have a heyday with her and Vince being here alone. In small towns, people didn't do that sort of thing until after marriage. At least, not unless they wanted to be the main topic of conversation.

Tugging her to her feet, Vince ran his hands beneath her shirt and up her sides, then cupped her breasts through her satin bra. "Just so you know, I intend to continue to see you and to hell with the grapevine if they don't approve."

Stretching her arms over her head, Hanna let him pull the shirt off. She wasn't ready to admit how much she wanted to spend every waking minute with this man. Correction, not just the waking minutes. "Yeah, you just wait until I find out all the things they've said about you. You might not be so cocky then."

"I've never set out to burn up the airwaves, but I'm not going to change my life just because your mother and her friends disapprove. I'm too old and I've been through too damn much. And I don't plan to let you get too caught up in it, either."

His shirt landed on the floor on top of hers. Then her bra. He pulled her tightly against him and started a seductive dance—bare chest to breasts, jeans to jeans. She hardly noticed the lack of music as she moved her hips with his and reveled at the touch of his calloused hands exploring her naked torso. The rub of his stubble as he nuzzled her breast and took her nipple into his mouth. His moist lips returned to hers and demanded attention as he hooked his thumbs into her waistband and slowed their moves to a sway.

Working their jeans off and adding them to the clothing pile, he opened his mouth across hers, exploring and melding her to him. He eased her down on the sofa and buried his hands in her hair, holding her face firm for a kiss.

"I tried not to worry about the grapevine when I was in high school. But every little thing made its way back to my mother before I even got home."

He backed away and stared at her. "So what did you do that warranted gossiping? Come on, you can't drop a bomb like that and not give details."

Hanna squealed as he tickled under her arms.

"I'm relentless until you give up every dirty little detail."

"Okay, okay." She tried to stop laughing long enough to catch her breath. "One night I went skinny-dipping in the lake with Freddie Smith. Old Man Thompson saw us and told Old Lady Thompson, who told Mrs. Haythorn, who couldn't wait to call Mom because of the whole Mom-spilling-the-beans-about-the-bun-in-the-oven thing, and Mrs. Haythorn had to get even. So by the time the story wound its way through the grapevine and I got home, my mother thought Freddie and I were going at it on the bank like rabbits. We just swam! Kissed a little. Why do old men fish at night anyway? That's asinine."

Vince's hand roamed over her belly and lower. "So I'm

messing around with a wild child! Good to know. Skinny-dipping. Maybe we should give that a try."

Her breath caught in her throat as she enjoyed his ministrations. "Oh come on, I'm sure you were wilder than I ever thought about being."

"No, I was studious. Had my eye on that engineering degree." His fingers kept up their ceaseless exploration. "I partied on occasion, but I was a good boy."

His stubble scratched her neck as he nuzzled lower toward her left breast. She cradled his head. "Oh you are very good."

Chapter Fifteen

Hanna woke up early and dressed. Still in her euphoria from the night before in Vince's arms, she left her mom and Ashton sleeping. She stuck a note on the fridge to let them know that she was opening the shop and there was no need for them to hurry this morning. She couldn't wipe the silly smile off her face at just the thought of making out with Vince. They were really going to give this thing between them a shot and suddenly all was right with the world.

The sky had just enough wispy clouds to make it pretty, and Hanna breathed in the fresh scents from the newly mown grass and spring flower beds. What a great day.

She stopped by the Barkley's corner store for a box of Mrs. Barkley's croissants on her way in. Nothing in the store had changed from the recently mopped well-worn beige vinyl floor to the tan metal shelves stocked with breakfast cereal. Hanna grinned at the red soda machine in the corner. Just as Dave had mentioned, the variety included those old-fashioned chocolate sodas she'd loved as a kid.

Mrs. Barkley handed her the box of croissants and her change. "Say hello to Norma for me." As they'd operated for forty-plus years, Mrs. Barkley got up before the sun came up every day and opened the store. She took care of the morning baking and Mr. Barkley ran the afternoon shift and closed up each night. The only difference in the woman was considerably more gray hairs than when Hanna had last seen her.

"Thanks, Mrs. Barkley. I will. Have a nice day."

Hanna had the coffee brewing and had already given in to the temptation of the heavenly aroma of fresh bread by the time her mother arrived.

Norma glided into the shop, wearing one of her dozen or so pairs of black slacks and today's blouse, a deep royal blue. Yep, it was Saturday. Always blue on Saturday. Her salt-and-pepper curls framed her narrow face like a helmet and with all that hairspray, they were probably about as soft.

"Morning, Mom. Is Ashton still asleep?"

"I cooked him breakfast, and he was sitting in front of the TV when I left. Said he'd be by in a little while."

Hanna was still getting used to her son being old enough to stay alone. "Croissants are on the counter."

"Anne Haythorn rang this morning. Seems she suspects her neighbor has a new lady friend."

"Oh, really?" Hanna grabbed some Hill Country brochures to refill the plastic rack and tried not to snap at her mother. True, they were from different generations. Yet her grandmother hadn't been a gossip, so that wasn't enough to sell Hanna on that excuse.

"She went over last night to take him a piece of pie, and he told her Kenzie was at her grandmother's house, but she could hear someone in the next room. And somebody was in the truck with him when he pulled in earlier that day."

Hanna slammed the stack of brochures on the counter. "Mom, I'm not trying to stir up the rumor mill, but I am going to live my life."

Norma shoved her glasses up on her nose and turned to face her daughter. "You have a son to think about, Hanna. How is this going to affect him?"

"Ashton likes Vince and vice versa."

"And if this relationship doesn't work out?" Norma paused for a breath. "That boy has been through enough."

Very true. "Mom, I don't want to argue about this. I enjoy Vince's company. And for now, that's enough reason for me to continue seeing him."

The bell on the front door jingled, and Anne Haythorn waltzed in. Her gray hair was cut in the latest style, in Hanna's opinion a tad too young for her, but who was she to judge?

"Good morning, Norma. Do you have that book I ordered for Molly? I was hoping it had come in before she arrives this afternoon." She turned her beaming smile on Hanna. "Hi, Hanna. I see a lot of that boy of yours at the Keegans."

"He and Kenzie are friends." Hanna pasted on her sweetest smile and walked over to the small coffee area. "Hot coffee? Croissant?"

"I guess I can spare a few minutes."

"There's sugar and creamer by the side. I'll just run and see if I can help Mom find that book."

Bluebonnet Books got incredibly busy as the spring tourists wandered in. Lots of people out for weekend excursions to see the wildflowers, and Norma managed to sell something to almost everyone who entered.

Ashton strolled in just before lunch with Kenzie in tow. Both kids had on faded jeans, T-shirts and backwards ball caps. "Mom, is it okay if we go to McDonald's for lunch?"

Hanna smiled at them. Neither she nor her mother had time to take off and make lunch for him. "Just a sec and I'll get you some cash."

She handed him the money and straightened a curl that had fallen across his forehead. "Be careful and watch for cars."

Ashton stuffed the money in his pocket. "We're walking today. Kenzie's bike has a flat. And if we have room after McDonald's, we may stop by Mr. Barkley's store for a chocolate soda."

A chocolate soda. Wow, kids still liked those? At least they were walking, with all the tourists adding to the traffic. "Have fun."

She was so busy when Vince called to ask her to lunch, she had to take the call while ringing out a customer. He waited until she was done, and Norma took over the register. Hanna eased her way back to the office for a minute's privacy. "I'm way too busy to take a lunch break today. Not that busy is a bad thing."

"No kidding. Kids tell you they were going to McDonald's?"

Hanna grinned. "They actually stopped by and asked permission for once. But you and I having lunch in public? Not such a good idea. Anyway, before we take this to the Falls Diner, we need to tell Kenzie and Ashton."

The line was quiet a minute. "Agreed. So we tell them after work tonight. Then I'll grab a bucket of fried chicken and some fishing gear and we'll pick you two up at seven."

Hanna frowned. "You don't waste any time do you? Think they might need an evening to adjust before we all go out?"

"They'll get used to the idea. Fishing will help. I don't think it'll surprise either of them too much anyway. See you tonight."

Vince hung up and dialed Gray. He wasn't happy about being turned down for lunch, but he did want to tell Kenzie before someone else did. God, last night with Hanna had been hot, but with Ashton at home, Hanna had left early. Alone time was going to be a challenge.

"Hey, bro. Got time to meet me at Mariah's shop and give me a lift home? I need to drop the Harley off for a tune-up. Might be a free lunch in it for you."

More like brothers than brothers-in-law, Vince and Gray covered each other's businesses when they needed time away.

And since it was a pretty equal trade-off, they never worried about money. Still, it wouldn't hurt to buy the guy lunch. Plus Vince was a little worried about Gray's reaction about seeing his brother-in-law with Hanna.

Vince parked the truck in the garage and straddled the Harley, ignoring the helmet on the shelf. He wanted the wind in his face today. Wanted to feel the power of the bike. Life was good. He and Hanna were both on the same page, at least enough to want to give this a shot. Kenzie was feeling better, and he had a date tonight.

When he pulled his Harley into the shop, his gaze landed on Mariah Calabrezie's jeans-covered rear end as she bent over a bike she was working on. Wiping her hands on a greasy rag, she straightened and flashed him a grin. Petite, pixie-faced, she looked like anything but a top-notch grease monkey.

"Hey, Vince. Harley got a problem?"

Vince put the kickstand down and got off. "Just came back from a short road trip. Engine's cutting out, idling rough."

Gray then pulled into the parking lot, but remained in the truck.

Mariah stared at the truck a second, but didn't comment. "May be a couple days before I can get to it. Springtime. Everyone wants to hit the road. Probably just needs a little TLC."

"No rush. You've got my cell number."

She nodded. "I'll call you after I get a chance to look at it."

He headed toward Gray's old, faded, green-and-white pickup. "What do you think about Mariah?"

"Thought you were hooking up with Hanna Rosser."

"Wasn't talking about me."

The truck door squeaked open and Gray flashed him a go-to-hell look. "Me and the biker lady? What are you smoking?"

"Mariah Calabrezie is the best damn mechanic this side of the Red River. This lady can make a bike hum like June bugs around a porch light."

Gray glanced at Mariah, but didn't seem too impressed. "Not the kind of woman to bring home for Mom's Sunday pot roast."

Vince was in a great mood and it seemed that a woman might be just what Grayson needed, as well. "So what is your type? Donna Reed?"

Gray ground the starter, but it took at least thirty seconds for the engine to kick in. "Lay off. There's nothing wrong with an old-fashioned woman who believes in the important things in life. The whole world is screwed up."

Vince raised an eyebrow and razzed him. "So you don't think a woman should work?"

Gray dropped the truck into first and growled. "Just saying that I don't understand why there aren't any women left who want to stay home and have babies. What happened to home and family?"

"Here's your problem." Suddenly all the pieces fell into place. "You have superwoman as a mom. How can any woman compare? Gardens, cooks, keeps the house clean, babysits the grandkids, mows the yard, there for everybody when they need her." Vince pointed toward the Falls Diner. "Lunch?"

Gray whipped the truck into the parking lot.

"Hell, I'm not sure I'd have ever gotten my act together after Belinda was killed without her support," Vince admitted.

"Exactly my point." Gray wedged the truck in between a Lexus and an F150 with a rack and ladders in the bed.

"You might want to whittle your requirements down to a more realistic list," Vince suggested.

"You keep hounding me like this and I'm going to order the biggest meal on the menu *and* dessert. So tell me about

Hanna Rosser. Things looked pretty chummy last night. And that chicken-eatin' grin has been plastered on your face since I pulled into the bike shop."

Vince cocked his head and wondered if Gray was as cool with this as he was acting. "Why don't you tell me what you think about Hanna?"

"She's a good person. I knew her in school." Gripping the wheel, Gray turned and stared at him. "Belinda's been dead a long time, Vince. You've got a life to live."

"Could say the same about you." Vince wasn't sure to what extent losing his twin had contributed to Gray's hang-ups about women.

"I miss her every damn day. She was my best friend." Gray flashed those white teeth. "But she'd kick our asses if she thought we weren't getting on with our lives."

"You got that right." For the first time in nine years Vince was actually beginning to realize that by his complete devotion to Kenzie and their life here, he'd closed himself off from some interesting possibilities. "When are you going to find a woman so I don't have to kick your ass for your sister?"

"When I'm damn good and ready. You buying me lunch?"

Vince slammed the pickup door and matched his stride to Gray's. "How about the secretary at the school? She asks about you almost every time I'm there." And that was more often than he'd have liked of late.

Gray shook his head. "Divorced. Two kids."

Vince snapped his finger. "Kim Martin. She's looking for somebody to be a daddy to her little girl. She'd love to stay home and have your babies."

Gray opened the door and walked into the diner. "I'm hungry. You hungry? Meat loaf smells good. I'm thinking banana cream pie."

AT LEAST THEY GOT TO finish their first course, but Vince had taken only two bites out of his pie when his cell phone rang. He glanced at the display.

"Hey, Ken—"

"Bully Baer's telling everybody that you're doing it with Ms. Rosser."

Vince dropped his fork onto the plate. "Kenzie, calm down."

"I know you broke up, so why's he being such a jerk and telling people that? I told him…"

Shit. "Kenzie, slow down a minute."

Silence. Frightening silence. "Are you and Ms. Rosser doing it?"

How was he supposed to handle this over the phone? He should have told her sooner. "Are you at McDonald's? Is Ashton still with you?"

A pause, then Ashton's gasp. "It's true?"

"Stay there and I'll pick you up."

"I don't want to stay here. And I don't want to talk to you. You told me it was over. You lied."

The phone went dead.

Now even the kids were being hurt by the town grapevine!

"We gotta go."

Without asking what was up, Gray started shoveling in bites of banana cream pie. Vince did the same with his coconut cream. "William Baer's boy told the kids about me and Hanna."

"That kid's a pain." Gray finished his pie and pushed in his chair.

Vince handed the waitress a couple bills, probably twice the cost of lunch, and followed Gray toward the truck. He dialed Hanna's phone. "We got a problem. Kids are upset. Billy Baer was at McDonald's and told them that you and I are sleeping together. Kenzie hung up on me. I don't know where they are."

Grayson made good time getting to the house. Vince really wasn't sure where Kenzie would go, but he needed his truck to find her.

"Back door's open," Gray said.

Vince bolted out of the truck. "You coming in?"

Gray shook his head. "This is between you and Kenzie."

"Yeah."

Vince didn't even get in the door before Kenzie pounced, hands on her hips. "So did Bully Baer lie? Or did you?"

Deep breath. "Hanna and I are dating."

Her blue eyes flashed. "You couldn't have just told us? You had to let that dweeb know before we did? He said you're—"

"Stop right there. This just happened. We planned to tell you tonight." Geez, it even sounded like a flimsy excuse to him.

Kenzie stomped up and huffed. "Well that's not soon enough." She pushed past him and flounced down on the sofa, arms crossed over her chest.

Vince squatted down in front of her, but she wouldn't even look at him. Tears glistened in her blue eyes. "Mackenzie, I did not lie to you." He bent his head and tried to capture her gaze. "When I told you Hanna and I weren't seeing each other, that was the truth. Things changed."

"Why do you need her anyway?" She sniffed and turned to face him. Instead of belligerence, he saw a hurt little girl.

"You're not a child anymore, Kenzie. In a few years you'll be going off to college. Probably get married and start your own life, and I want the best life possible for you. I want all your dreams to come true." He waited and let that register. "But where does that leave me?"

She shrugged.

"No matter where each of our lives lead, nothing can lessen what we have. You'll always be my little girl and nobody can come between us."

"But why Ash's mom?"

"I enjoy her company. Would you rather me date somebody who had a kid you didn't like?"

At least she finally uncrossed her arms. "No, but she's sort of a pain."

"She's been through a lot just like Ashton has. She's entitled to a little time to adjust before you start making judgments."

"What happens when you break up? It'll make it hard for me and Ash to be friends. Have you thought about that? I like hanging out with him."

"And I like hanging out with Hanna. So let's give this a try. It could work out well for all of us."

"I'm not so sure about that."

VINCE CHECKED THE TACKLE BOX to make sure they weren't forgetting anything.

Kenzie jammed her pink cap on backwards and grabbed the fishing poles. "It'll be a hoot to watch Ashton fish, but tell me again why his mom's going? She doesn't seem like the fishing type."

"Because I want her to." Vince tossed the tackle box and a blanket into the truck bed and slammed the tailgate.

Kenzie smirked, then clapped her hands at the dog. "Come on Boo. Let's go."

Vince started the truck and Boo leaped into the backseat. "Just so we're straight, Kenzie. I expect you to be nice to Hanna. Show some respect."

"Whatever."

HANNA WASN'T SURPRISED that Ashton didn't have the least issue with the dating situation. His only concern was Billy

Baer and how Kenzie was taking it. When Vince and Kenzie pulled up, he bolted into the truck and rubbed Boo's head. "Hey, boy."

Vince held the door for Hanna, and grinned at the boy and the dog's slobbery greeting.

Wearing jeans and a black T-shirt, Vince looked even more sexy than usual. She wondered if he'd kiss her hello, but he didn't. She was glad they were thinking alike, that maybe it was best to take it slow, give the kids time to adjust.

"Hi, Mackenzie," Hanna said, hoping to get some feel for how tonight was going to work.

"Hi," Mackenzie replied, then turned her attention to Ashton and began rattling off a thousand details about fishing.

Vince slid into the cab and leaned forward for a kiss. "You ever fish?"

Taken by surprise, she touched her tongue to her lip and narrowed her eyes. "Not since I was young and Daddy took me. Let's just say that I was not a natural at the sport."

After a quick stop by the sporting goods store for licenses and a run to KFC for a bucket of chicken, they were off to the lake.

Mackenzie grabbed the chicken and staked out the concrete picnic table closest to the water. Ashton took the blanket and Hanna grabbed the drinks while Vince brought up the rear hauling the fishing gear. Boo didn't even slow down at the table, just headed straight for the water's edge to sniff around.

Please let this evening be a success. Hanna knew Mackenzie had a lot of pull with her father and she was the best friend Ashton had ever had. Hanna wanted to get along.

"Dinner first." Vince stopped Kenzie in her tracks as she started toward the water.

"Dad, can't we fish a few minutes, then eat?"

"Chicken's hot and you might want to eat before you get fish guts on your hands."

"Good point," Ashton said.

Hanna had never seen Ashton wolf down his food so fast. But Kenzie still beat him. She handed Boo the last bite of chicken, tossed her empty plate into the garbage and grabbed a rod and reel. "I'll be over there on the dock."

"Stay in sight."

"Wait up!" Ashton tossed his plate and looked at the other three rods. "Which one do I use?"

"The green one."

Ashton took off after Mackenzie and Boo, trying to run and hold the rod up.

"Ashton's okay with this?"

Hanna shrugged and watched a boat with two fisherman putt across the mirror-smooth lake toward the docks on the opposite shore, leaving a narrow wake behind. "Thought it was kind of cool. What about Kenzie?"

"Kenzie will get a grip."

Hanna certainly hoped so, but she wasn't sure. "And let's hope Bully Baer stays out of her path until after she does."

"No kidding." Vince smiled at Hanna. "What else is wrong?"

She gulped. He could read her way too well. She hadn't even told her mother this. "Ashton told me that Richard's law-student girlfriend is pregnant."

Vince didn't seem to grasp the gravity of that. "Good. Maybe he'll be preoccupied with the new baby and not have time to pressure you about Ashton."

"Evidently Ashton has known for a month or two and they asked him to keep it quiet because she's due in August."

"Which means she was pregnant when he asked for a divorce?"

"Yeah." Her voice cracked. She wasn't sure why the confirmation had hit her so hard. "I'd guessed she might be pregnant when Richard asked for a divorce, but he denied it."

Vince ran his palm down her cheek.

She swiped an escaped tear. "God, I hate him right now. Why do men think with their… Why can't they use their brains?"

"I'm sorry. That's gotta hurt." He ran a thumb under her eye.

"No, I'm sorry. I didn't mean to throw you into the scumbag category with my ex. It just seems so sleazy. This girl is so young, she was still living at home with her parents. She's only ten years older than Ashton. How sick is that!"

Vince looked at the kids, then back at Hanna. "What does Ashton think about a baby brother or sister?"

"That's how Ashton slipped and told me. He went with them shopping for baby furniture during spring break. They're redecorating the bedroom that was my office with new pink baby furniture." She felt like bursting into tears. "It's so stupid, but that room was mine. It's not logical to feel this violated over a dumb room."

He slid an arm around her. "There's nothing stupid about it. It was your room. Your home."

"Winnie the Pooh is going to be living in my cherrywood study. And I'm living with my mother and sleeping in the stupid white canopy bed I got when I was eight."

"Well, I could suggest a solution for the bed issue, but you might surmise that I was rushing things." He stood and tugged her to her feet. "Come on. Fishing soothes the soul."

She knew he was kidding about moving in, but the idea of the four of them sharing a house, of her sleeping in Vince's arms each night didn't frighten her nearly as much as it should have.

Vince tied a lure onto the line and demonstrated how to cast. When Hanna took the fishing rod from him and gave it a try, the lure dropped to the ground at her feet, not even close to landing in the lake. "Fishing's not really my thing."

Mackenzie rolled her eyes, but Vince was facing Hanna and didn't notice. Hanna was tempted to stick her tongue out, but instead put more determination into the next cast and at least landed it in the water with a tiny splash. Mackenzie didn't seem to notice, as she and Ashton were giggling about something.

Hanna frowned when Vince's line sailed past hers and landed in the middle of the lake. "That's what you expect me to do?"

He laid down his fishing rod, slipped one arm around her back and put his hand over hers on the handle. "I've got confidence in you. Try this."

Backing into his chest, she held the fishing rod and moved her arm with his, enjoying the unison of their body movement. She released the button on the reel and the line soared out over the lake. The lure dropped into the water with a gentle splash.

"I caught one." Mackenzie bounced from one sneaker to the other as she reeled in the fish.

Reluctantly Hanna felt the absence of Vince's warmth as he turned toward Mackenzie. She had to confess that she was impressed when instead of waiting for Vince to do it, Mackenzie removed the fish from the hook and held it up for Ashton's approval. Not a glimpse of squeamishness.

"Whoa! Look at that one. He's got to be at least a five-pounder," Ashton assured her.

Hanna studied the tiny fish. They'd be lucky if it weighed a pound.

"Unless you plan to catch a bunch more and treat everyone to a fish fry, you might want to toss him back now." Vince nodded toward the water.

"You don't eat them?" Hanna stared at him in bemusement as Mackenzie gently knelt down and released the fish.

"Sometimes, but mostly we just fish for fun and let them go."

"It doesn't hurt them?"

"Nah, they just get harder to catch next time. Just adds challenge to the game."

"You're an interesting man, Mr. Keegan."

He flashed those dimples and dug his ringing cell phone out of his jeans. "Hey, Claire."

Hanna cast her line and tried not to eavesdrop.

"No use in Greg driving all the way up from Fredericksburg. And like you said, Gray is a master at the lawn, but when it comes to anything mechanical he's useless. I'll drop by tomorrow sometime and take a look." He paused. "Have you ever known me to turn down a home-cooked meal?" He laughed. "Yeah, tell the guys they're off the hook this time. See you around noon."

It was dusk when they wrapped up the adventure. On another evening Hanna would have put the fishing rod aside and just enjoyed the breathtaking sunset and sounds of frogs croaking and water lapping against the shore, but tonight she wasn't about to give Mackenzie any reason to think she couldn't hold her own. She kept casting that silly rod until the rest of them started packing up.

"So where are we going tomorrow?" Ashton tossed his rod into the pickup bed with the others.

"We're staying home and doing homework. You two aren't out of school yet," Hanna stated. Vince obviously had plans with the Maguires and Hanna didn't want him to feel as if he had to entertain them every evening.

Both kids groaned as they piled back into the pickup for the short trip home.

Vince held Hanna's arm and gave it a squeeze as she

climbed into the tall truck. She felt a warm rush when he winked before closing her door.

"But tomorrow's Sunday. What if we get our homework done early?" Kenzie asked. "Then we could go see the new movie that started yesterday."

"I got most of mine done at school anyway," Ashton chimed in. "So I vote for the movie."

"You heard your mom. Sunday is a school night."

"Then maybe Ash could come to our house in the afternoon and we could do homework and play the Wii?"

The fact that she wasn't mentioned in that invite did not go unnoticed by Hanna. "Not tomorrow. Ashton takes his grades very seriously."

Ashton sat up straight. "I take the Wii seriously, too, and last time she beat me, so I have to prove she's not better than me."

"I am better than you." Mackenzie punched Ashton. "You need to work on your swing and quit wasting all your energy trying to figure out how the game works."

"Oh, you are going to pay for that. I'm going to beat you so bad."

Vince turned onto the road and shook his head. "No Wii until all homework is done and we give permission." He high-fived Hanna. "Parents rule. *Ah-ah-ah-ah-ah!*" He sounded very much like the Count on *Sesame Street*.

Kenzie frowned. "Great. Your mom is wearing off on my dad. What's up with that?"

Ashton groaned. "That sucks green pond scum."

Chapter Sixteen

If members of the grapevine had any doubts, they wouldn't in five minutes. During the Monday lunch hour at Falls Dinner, Vince put a possessive hand on Hanna's back. If they were going to do this, they might as well put it out in the open and squelch speculation. In nine years in Marble Falls, he'd dated, even dated in "public," but had never brought anyone to Falls Diner at lunch when the entire town was likely to be there.

He felt Hanna take a deep breath. As she glanced up at him, he smiled. "They won't have nearly as much to gossip about if we're not sneaking around."

She nodded and led the way into the café.

Vince's mouth watered at the aroma of home-cooking permeating the bustling café. He took off his cap and escorted Hanna to a seat at a booth next to the counter.

The waitress grinned as she placed their menus on the Formica-topped table. "Hanna Creed. I wondered how long it'd take you to wander through here."

Vince tried not to laugh at the blank expression on Hanna's face. She had no idea what the woman's name was. "Hey, Penny. What's the special today?" he asked, hoping to help Hanna out.

"Chicken-fried steak and homemade mashed potatoes."

Hanna grinned. "Penny Jones. It's been a long time."

Penny laughed and patted Hanna's hand. "Dave Barkley

told me you'd moved back. I wondered when you'd get around to stopping by and saying hello. Lots of people leave and return, but I figured you would be the last person to move back."

"I should have kept in touch." Hanna tried to not take Penny's remark personally, but she was right. She and Penny had been friends; but at eighteen, while Penny had been planning a wedding, Hanna had been counting down the days until she could trade in small-town U.S.A. for an exciting life in the big city.

Penny placed napkin-rolled flatware on the table. "My daughter said your boy and Kenzie had become fast friends." She looked between Vince and Hanna as if wondering if it was only the kids who'd gotten close.

Vince was fascinated by Hanna's baffled expression. She moved her glass to the other side of her place mat, then back. "They are. Kenzie has done wonders helping Ashton adjust."

"And how are you adjusting to living back in Marble Falls? I'm sure we must seem pretty boring after living in Dallas."

Hanna's gaze shifted to Vince. "I'm settling in quite nicely, thanks. And that chicken-fried steak sounds wonderful. Do you have baby carrots?"

"We do." Penny didn't even write the order down, just turned and grinned at Vince.

"I'll have the same, plus a glass of iced tea."

"Make that two," Hanna said.

As Penny bustled off to place their order, skillfully dodging another waitress balancing a tray of desserts, Vince chuckled. "Well, it's all but official now."

"Oh my gosh, I sure hope we know what we're doing here." Hanna's cheeks blushed an adorable rosy pink.

"Now that you mention it, there is one thing I'm trying to figure out. How the hell are we going to get any time alone with two kids?" Vince wasn't willing to have Hanna sleep over with Kenzie in the house any more than she was willing with Ashton in town. Spring break only came once a year and that wasn't going to cut it. "Does Ashton go to his dad's this weekend?"

She sat back and smiled as Penny placed two glasses of iced tea on the table. "We swapped weekends, so Ashton isn't going until the weekend after. It's Richard's birthday and he wants Ashton there."

"Is it getting any easier to let him go?" Vince took a drink of tea. He knew it had torn her up in the beginning.

Her jaw set as she squeezed lemon into her iced tea. "How would you handle another man interfering with raising Mackenzie?"

"I'd have to kill him."

Hanna took a drink and chuckled. "No, you wouldn't. If anything went wrong, Mackenzie would cause a ruckus...be in his face so fast he'd never want to have any part of raising her again."

He laughed. "True. But you might underestimate Ashton. He can stand up for himself."

"I hope so. He's a smart kid, just keeps his emotions buried."

Probably way too buried for his own good. "Kenzie doesn't bury anything, except maybe the bodies."

"A person knows where she stands with that girl."

"Just like her mother." He quirked an eyebrow. "Thanks for making the effort to get along with her. She can be a challenge."

Hanna twirled a dark curl around her finger. "I'm hoping she'll come around. And if she does, maybe I'll have fewer issues with Ashton."

"Ashton will settle in."

The waitress plunked their food in front of them, and Hanna

picked up her fork and focused those dark eyes on him. "Are you really so sure of everything?"

Jake Watson clapped Vince on the shoulder as he and Dave Barkley walked by on their way to a table. "How goes it, Vince? Keeping out of trouble?"

"Where's the fun in that?" Vince asked the older men.

Jake tipped his worn, straw cowboy hat at Hanna. "Ma'am." He rolled the rim of the hat in his hand and cocked a crooked grin at Dave. "The boy might have a point there."

Dave didn't seem to hear Jake's remark. "Aren't you Norma Creed's girl? The one that scooted out of here for Dallas when you was still wet behind the ears? Heard you were back."

Hanna swallowed her bite of chicken-fried steak and nodded at Dave. "That's right, Mr. Barkley. I used to buy candy and pop at your grocery store."

Dave beamed. "You were fond of those chocolate sodas, weren't ya?"

"Wow, I can't believe you remember that. Couldn't get full of them." Her eyes sparkled.

"I've still got some cold ones in the chest. You just stop on by."

Vince frowned at the older man. "You trying to make time with my lunch date there, Dave?"

"Smart boy shouldn't turn his back on ol' Dave with a beautiful lady around." Jake winked at Vince, then shuffled off toward the table where the waitress had placed their menus.

"Small towns." Hanna shook her head as Claire Maguire suddenly bustled through the front door, a huge turquoise-and-silver hobo purse hanging off her right arm.

"Hello, Vince." Claire hugged Vince's shoulder. Her smile faded into a wrinkled brow. "Hanna."

"Mrs. Maguire."

The older woman flashed a motherly grin at Vince. "I ran

in for some groceries. Thought I'd pick up a big apple pie for dinner. You and Kenzie are coming over tonight, right?"

"Sure."

"And the monthly family BBQ on Sunday? James and Jen are coming in from Austin with the kids."

Vince glanced at Hanna. He'd rather spend the day with her and Ashton, but he hated to hurt Claire's feelings. Besides Kenzie would be ticked if she missed seeing her cousins.

Claire stared at him, then across the table at Hanna. "You're welcome to bring guests."

"Um, that's up to Hanna." He didn't know how not to put her on the spot, but he was pretty sure she'd rather not go. "Do we have anything planned Sunday?"

Hanna put down her fork. "No. It's up to you."

"Then it's settled. We'll expect you around noon." Claire hugged Vince, waved at Hanna and walked over to the counter to order her pie.

Hanna did not look pleased. "I'm sorry about that," Vince said.

Both eyebrows rose and she blew out a breath. "It's okay. I'd sort of hoped we could put that off until we were a little further along."

"They're nice folks and there'll be a crowd. Gray for one, and you like him. The kids will have fun fishing and swimming."

Hanna forked a carrot. "Yeah."

HANNA WASN'T LOOKING FORWARD to the afternoon at the Maguire house, but at least she'd get to spend time with Vince. Still, it was going to be awkward at best. Ashton was certainly psyched. He had his swimsuit and towel packed. He'd called Mackenzie to remind her to bring him a fishing rod and the life jacket for the boat Mackenzie kept at her grandparents' dock. The Keegans were becoming his personal social directors.

The quick kiss from Vince when he picked them up was about as close to intimacy as the day presented. Vince unloaded a huge chest of iced-down sodas from the truck, and Kenzie and Ashton hauled it around back to the deck. Hanna picked up the spinach salad she'd made and followed Vince up the walk. The flower bed overflowed with bright multicolored impatiens—red, purple, white and pink. The one closest to the porch sported a bunch of daisies. Perfect picture of a family home.

A group of boys tossed a Frisbee across the manicured front yard. "Hey, Uncle Vince!" one yelled, tossing him the fluorescent-orange disk.

Vince snagged it out of the air and tossed it back. "Hey, guys. This is Hanna."

"Hey, Hanna," one said, spinning and tossing the Frisbee to one of the others from behind his back.

Hanna stepped onto the porch of the ranch-style home. A couple of men waved from two of the rockers on the porch that extended the full length of the house. "Vince, you need to get out back before Wayne burns the burgers."

Vince grinned. "And you guys weren't man enough to keep him away from the grill?"

"Supervising the grill is your job."

"Yeah, yeah." Vince held the door open for Hanna.

Hanna set the spinach salad on the dining table already laden with a host of other dishes. The house was full of women, all working together like ants in a colony. Everyone moved around the huge, country-style kitchen, dodging as drawers and cabinet doors were opened, balancing dishes as they zigzagged about the room.

"Everyone, this is my friend Hanna Rosser." Vince flashed a grin and hugged a couple of the women.

"Remember Hanna Creed?" Grayson arrived just behind them. "She was a year younger than me and Belinda in school."

Hanna smiled at the tiny white-haired woman by his side. Gray took the dish out of the older woman's hand and placed it on the sideboard. "Hanna, this is our grandmother."

Shaking the frail hand, Hanna smiled. "Nice to meet you. That peach cobbler smells wonderful."

The large sprawling house oozed with the four Maguire boys and their families. Hanna was introduced to so many people, she couldn't keep track of them. Belinda's three older brothers were all tall and dark-haired. All were married and had kids, although she wasn't sure who had how many and which kids belonged to which family. Some of the women who introduced themselves to her or to whom she was introduced, didn't even appear to be family members. But like the other women, they all seemed to be used to the routine of the Maguire kitchen.

Vince left her to the crowd and made his way to the grill on the back deck. The Maguire's manicured lawn sloped gently down to the wooden boat dock, crowded with people, yet tranquil and oozing family camaraderie. Hanna watched as Vince's father-in-law clapped him on the back and handed him the tongs for the grill. Kids fished off the dock while others pedaled around the lake in two paddleboats. An older boy glided up to the deck on a Jet Ski.

The routine appeared to be that the men kept an eye on the kids and manned the large smoker and grill while the women hung out in the kitchen and caught up on family happenings.

Other than that, Hanna wasn't exactly sure how the kitchen organization worked. Everyone else obviously felt right at home as they pulled dishes out of the various cabinets and flatware out of drawers. One woman peeled potatoes and another buttered and wrapped corn in foil for the grill. It was like a well-orchestrated, chaotic play as each woman took care of business. Every time Hanna tried to help, someone else was already on top of it.

Wandering into the homey family room, Hanna browsed the pictures on the mantel. Belinda in a pep-squad uniform. A family portrait when the four boys and Belinda were in high school. A framed snapshot of Vince, Belinda and the kids at Sea World. Wedding portraits, including Vince and Belinda's.

"He's a good man. One of us," Grandma said from behind her shoulder. "He and Belinda were an interesting match. Good parents."

Hanna smiled, her gaze landing back on Vince's wedding portrait. Belinda was holding a bouquet of yellow and white daisies. "Belinda carried daisies at her wedding."

"From the time she was little, Belinda loved the yellow and white daisies that grew in my yard." Her grandmother said. "Always picking a bouquet and bringing them inside." Grandma kissed her finger and touched it to the photo. "I think they represented her happy, sunny personality."

Hanna's heart hit bottom as she smiled at the older woman, then glanced back at the pictures, many of which showed Vince. The reality of how much of Belinda was infused into every aspect of Vince's life stung. This was the Vince etched in Claire Maguire's mind.

Hanna ran a finger down the smooth silver picture frame of Vince's past. She smiled at Belinda's diminutive grandmother when what she really felt like doing was having a good cry. "Vince is a good guy."

Grandma nodded. "Rather attentive to that boy of yours, too."

"He is." Hanna turned away from the pictures and faced her. "And Ashton is one of his biggest fans." Which probably wasn't good. As fond as Vince was of Ashton, Hanna would never penetrate the strong hold Belinda's memory still had on him. And she wasn't willing to play second fiddle.

Scrutinizing her, Grandma looked back at the pictures on the mantel. Hanna waited for her to speak, but she just shook her head and wandered out of the room as quietly as she'd wandered in.

Uncomfortable, Hanna returned to the kitchen and finally found a job helping haul paper plates, plastic dinnerware and huge bowls of food out to the picnic tables on the patio and lawn.

Hanna smiled at Ashton tossing a Frisbee with Mackenzie and another boy. She could only wish she was doing half as well with the women. They smiled and were genuinely friendly, but they all were in sync with the family dynamics. At any given time at least three conversations were fighting for air space around Hanna, leaving her at loose ends. Not that it seemed intentional, but she was odd man out.

Vince and three other men were sitting on lawn chairs beside the grill, laughing and carrying on.

This family obviously felt that Vince Keegan was one of them, and from what she'd observed, he shared that sentiment.

She leaned against the deck railing to check on Ashton and Grayson came up beside her. "Hey, Hanna."

"Quite an impressive operation you have here," she said.

"You look overwhelmed." Without the ball cap Gray usually wore, he looked more like the boy she remembered from high school. Dark-brown hair and smoky eyes, chiseled features. Not bad at all.

"Want me to track down Vince to save you from the insanity? They're almost too much for me and most of 'em are family." He flashed white teeth and pointed to a scrawny kid in a lime-green swimsuit who jumped and snagged a Frisbee.

"That one belongs to my cousin Charlie—or my other cousin Dan. I'm never sure."

She laughed. "So you're not exactly a family guy?"

"I love 'em all, one at a time." He raised a dark eyebrow. "But all at once?"

"I can relate." At Grayson's age, it was funny he wasn't married. He could have been through a bad divorce, but then again, she might just be equating his loneliness to her recent situation.

Ashton and Mackenzie sat on the edge of the dock, dangling their feet in the water and fishing with the boy they'd been tossing the Frisbee with earlier.

Hanna studied Vince and the other guys and how they laughed and joked. Grilling ribs, hot dogs and hamburgers. Taking turns carousing with the kids. Vince was just as much a part of this family as if he'd been born into it.

Loaded down with yet more food, Claire Maguire approached the kitchen door. Hanna rushed to hold it open for her. "Here, let me take one of those bowls."

Claire continued to balance the food. "I've got it, but thanks for getting the door."

Not giving his mother any choice, Gray reached for the bowl of green beans. Claire smiled and relinquished her hold. "Thanks, sweetie."

Again, Hanna was left at loose ends. Gritting her teeth, she went back inside and offered to help one of the sisters-in-law scoop potato salad into a serving dish.

Maybe after lunch she could find an excuse to escape.

But later, Ashton wanted to go swimming and refused to leave before getting wet. Vince took all four of their plates and tossed them into a plastic garbage sack, then started gathering up more trash. Hanna smiled at him and helped clear off the tables.

He gave her a quick kiss on the cheek. "I've got to help the guys clean up the grill. Relax and watch the kids." He had no clue how uncomfortable she was in Belinda's mother's home. And the Maguire home was truly a home full of love, just not for the new girlfriend of their late daughter's husband.

By the time the afternoon festivities finally wound down, Hanna was done. She'd tried to fit in and some of the other women were friendly enough, but Claire tended to stay in another room or talked to someone else. Trying to put herself in the woman's place, Hanna didn't push it. Claire Maguire was probably just as uncomfortable as Hanna was.

Vince didn't seem to notice Claire's reluctance to include Hanna. He pulled her into a game of Frisbee and on a boat ride around Lake Marble Falls with Mackenzie, Ashton and two of the nephews. Vince took it easy, just cruising around the lake on the pontoon boat. They stopped in a cove and let the kids swim. That part of the day was enjoyable at least. Hanna was so intent on watching the kids swim that when Vince sat beside her, she jumped.

"You having fun?"

She shrugged. "It's so peaceful out here. The kids love it."

Leaning around, he gave her a sweet kiss. "Sorry if I've ignored you today. I get so tangled up in everything going on, I forget you aren't used to all the chaos."

The chaos wasn't what bothered her. What Vince couldn't see was that Claire still considered him to be Belinda's husband. The woman was cordial, but the thought of accepting a new girlfriend into Vince's life was tearing Claire apart. Hanna received the nonverbal message Claire sent out loud and clear. The Maguires were his family in spirit if not in fact. And Hanna couldn't ask Vince to choose between her and his family. It was a no-win situation.

By the time Vince dropped her and Ashton off at home,

she was drained. Vince kissed her, but she pulled back. "It's late and I need to get Ashton into bed."

He narrowed one eye. "Okay."

Ashton finished his shower and she'd just kissed him good-night when her cell phone rang. Assuming it was Vince, she didn't even look at the display. "Hey there."

"Hey," Richard's voice answered.

"Oh. Hi. I… Just a minute and I'll get the phone to Ashton before he goes to sleep. He just crawled into bed."

"I called to talk to you."

Still dressed for the cookout, Hanna's mood was about as rank as her sweaty shirt. "Okay."

"I've been doing a lot of thinking, Hanna. I made a serious mistake. There is no excuse for what I did to you and to our family. I love you. I always have. I love Ashton. What can I say to get you to come home?"

Chapter Seventeen

Dropping onto the edge of the bed, Hanna could barely think. "Come home? After everything you've done? The things you said?"

"It was a moment of weakness. Phoebe came on to me. She looked up to me like you hadn't in years," Richard said.

Hanna honestly couldn't imagine how to respond.

"Are you still there? Please don't hang up."

She should hang up. She should throw the phone so far across the room that it would shatter into a million pieces. But right this minute, the thought of putting all the changes over the past few months behind her and going back into her world sounded almost tempting. "I'm here."

"Did Ashton tell you that Phoebe is pregnant?"

"Yes."

"Of course I'll support the baby, but Phoebe's moved home with her parents. It just isn't working. She doesn't know how to take care of herself, much less a baby or Ashton. She's excited about having a baby, but not about raising one. She's focused on finishing law school."

"Did she leave or did you ask her to leave?"

"She was too emotional to discuss things rationally so I talked to her father. He's a senior lawyer in the firm and it just seemed that it was best if we worked things out. I think

Phoebe was relieved. She isn't ready to be married and have a twelve-year-old stepson."

Hanna felt a slow burn in her chest. "So it didn't work with her, and now you want me back? Well, screw you." She disconnected. What she wouldn't give for a good old-fashioned phone, one she could slam down. Punching the tiny green Off button didn't give her anger nearly enough release. She paced, grabbed her old rag doll off the shelf and flung it against the wall. "Damn him!"

The bedroom door opened and her mother peeped around. "Are you okay?"

"No! That was Richard."

"And?"

Hanna took a deep breath and let it out. Took another and finally stared at her mother. "He figured out that he doesn't want to raise his young girlfriend *and* the baby, so now he wants me to come home." She fought to steady her breathing. "How can he possibly think I'd just come back as if nothing had happened? As if he'd done nothing wrong?"

"So you prefer to stay in Marble Falls? Make Bluebonnet Books work? Keep seeing Vince?"

"Two out of three maybe."

Norma came fully into the room and sat on the bed. "Not a good day?"

"What was I thinking?" Hanna scrubbed her face. "Men are too much work, and rushing into this thing with Vince is a mistake until I resolve my anger around Richard. At the moment, my feminine ego is still too bruised."

Hanna plopped down on the bed and Norma wrapped a motherly arm around her shoulders. "It'll all work out."

"Even if I decided to take on Vince's daughter, mother-in-law and the Marble Falls grapevine for his affections, I don't stand a chance in hell against a ghost."

Norma kissed the top of her head. "You always have a home here. Take all the time you need to figure things out."

Hanna's cell chimed again and this time she checked the display. "It's Vince." The phone bounced as she tossed it onto the bed unanswered. "I'm taking a long hot soak in the tub."

VINCE DIDN'T GET TOO worked up about Hanna not answering her phone on Sunday night until she still didn't answer twice on Monday. But when she still hadn't returned his messages Tuesday morning, he swung by Bluebonnet Books to see what was up. Obviously she hadn't had much fun at the Maguires' barbecue, but that didn't explain why she was suddenly not talking to him.

As he entered the store, he spotted her sitting in a short blue chair designed for children, helping a mother and little boy in the children's section. She glanced up at him, but didn't leave her customers. He snagged the latest copy of *Field and Stream* off the rack and thumbed through it.

He didn't see Norma, so hoped that when Hanna finished with the customer, they could actually talk in private. The beauty of being self-employed meant he didn't have to punch a clock. So until she talked to him, he wasn't leaving.

Finally the lady selected some books for their trip to Houston. The boy was stepping high and smiling when they left, swinging the bag with his new books in one hand and holding his mom's hand with the other.

Vince waited for the door to click shut before he spoke. "Cute kid. Now, care to tell me what's wrong?"

Hanna twisted a curl and avoided his eyes. Not a positive sign.

"Hanna, talk to me. Did I do something wrong?"

"No." Those sad, dark eyes closed. "You did everything right, maybe too right."

"What the hell does that mean?"

"It means I've been divorced only a few months and you're Mr. Perfect. Your charm is quite disarming. I needed to feel desirable, like I wasn't a loser in the romance department, and you waltzed in with all that slow Southern cool and voilà."

His throat tightened. "We're back to that old timetable thing?"

"I have to get myself straight before I'm going to be in any shape to contribute to a relationship. There are things I've got to deal with on my own first."

What the hell wasn't she saying? Something had happened. "Was it the barbecue?"

"The Maguires are nice people. The bazillion of them. They love you and Mackenzie, and that's fantastic."

"They'll love you, too."

"No, they won't. I don't belong there any more than I belong in a relationship right now. I don't know what I was thinking. Or maybe I just wasn't."

"Hanna, you know what they went through losing Belinda. What I went through." He'd opened his heart to this woman. Shared his darkest moments with her. Was that it? Did that scare her? "Give them time."

"You need to give *me* time. It took you nine years to get here. To work through your issues and be open to a relationship. It's just been a few months for me. My wounds are still bleeding. I have to figure out…"

Suddenly it hit him. "Richard back in the picture?"

"I would never go back to Richard."

"Really?"

"I have a son to think about. The last thing he needs is to start relying on you and then have you reject him like his father did. He couldn't handle that."

Vince's head spun. "First off, your son is stronger than you give him credit for. And second, the one being rejected here is me. You're throwing away a good thing on the offhand chance that it might not work out. And that makes zero sense."

Tossing the magazine on the rack, Vince was so angry he was almost vibrating. "If you ever get ready to tell me what's really going on here, you've got my number."

"Vince, I'm not trying to hurt you."

"Hurt me?" Turning, he was tempted to shake her—or kiss her—until she came to her senses, but who was he kidding? For whatever reason, she'd made up her mind. "I'm fine! Hell. That's just the way us country boys roll, right?"

He'd never been one for slamming doors, but he'd have liked nothing better than making the windows rattle when he left the bookstore. Of course, Hanna had one of those springs on the door that closed it slowly, and he would have had to break the contraption to get a resounding slam out of it. So he got in the truck and slammed that door instead.

Whatever the hell was eating Ms. Rosser, he could only hope it would pass in time. Maybe he'd rushed things. Whatever it was, he'd gotten one message loud and clear—she didn't want him in her life.

AFTER WORK, HE RAN by the house to pick up Kenzie and treat her to pizza. He'd been on his own a long time and he refused to brood over Hanna Rosser.

But as he pulled into the drive, Mrs. Haythorn stood up from working in her flower bed. She waved, sprinting toward him before he even got out of the truck.

"Hi, Vincent. Hope you had a good day. Mackenzie's in the house. Said she had math homework. How is Hanna today?"

He did not need Mrs. H. fishing for any juicy details she could spread around town. "Hanna is fine. Was that Dave Barkley's red pickup I saw in your drive this morning after Mr. Haythorn left for work?"

"Well, uh, y-yes." She stammered and looked slightly off center at having the tables turned. "This old house has shifted and he's working on the doors."

The stammer in her voice was just what he was going for. Busybody. He was tired of everyone knowing his business. Maybe he had sold out by moving here. Maybe it was time to consider a change. "Hope Dave takes care of everything for you."

KENZIE PILED HER PLATE with pizza from the buffet and slid into the red vinyl booth facing him. "So today when I dropped Ashton off, Ms. Rosser was in a tiff. She barked at him to get right on his homework and didn't even speak to me."

"Does she typically speak to you?"

Biting into a slice, Kenzie shrugged and swallowed. "Yeah, she's been offering me a cookie or brownie or whatever they have for the customers."

"Maybe it was a busy day."

"There was a plate of sugar cookies beside the coffeepot." Kenzie stared him in the eye. "Something's wrong or she and Ash would be here with us."

Great, he was being quizzed by a twelve-year-old. If Kenzie had picked up on it, the grapevine would, too. Who the hell cared? "We're not going to hang out with Hanna and Ashton for a while."

Kenzie narrowed one eye. "Uh-oh."

"Hanna just needs some time. No big deal." Like hell, but he wasn't about to tell Kenzie that.

"That's cool. It's always been just you and me, kid." She winked as she quoted his stock line every time life dealt them a blow.

He reached over and tweaked her nose. "Think you're pretty smart, don't you?"

"Grandma said that you should always put me first anyway. So this works out."

What? He'd always put Kenzie before anything and everything. "Why would she say that?"

Kenzie slurped her soda. "Oh, she always says that. She thinks you're an awesome father because you always want what's best for me."

"Of course I want what's best for you, but why would you or Grandma ever think Hanna or anyone else would change that?"

"I don't. Just saying." She pushed her empty plate aside. "I need more pizza. Want me to bring you another slice of pepperoni?"

Vince ate so much he practically had pizza sauce coming out his ears as they headed toward the truck. Kenzie wrapped her arm around his waist and jabbed her left foot in front of his.

He returned the favor and they continued on their way as they always had. Just him and the kid. That wasn't so bad. It was simple. But one of these days he was going to end up alone. One lonely rocker on the damn front porch.

If there was ever a time he needed the Harley, it was now. First thing tomorrow he'd call Mariah and see if it was ready. Maybe after school finished next weekend he'd drop Kenzie at his folks and just take off somewhere. Anywhere. Hell, maybe he'd take her with him. Call it a graduation trip.

Women! How could he have been so wrong about Hanna? There was one element of relationships he did not miss and that was their total unpredictability.

He started the truck and turned to Kenzie. "When you grow up and get a boyfriend, if you have a problem with him, just tell him straight out what you think. We don't know how to fix things if you don't tell us what's wrong. Got that?"

The cutest little wrinkle formed between her eyes. "Got it, Dad. Wow, you're really hung up on Ms. Rosser, huh?"

"No." The kid should not be this smart at twelve. "I just do not understand the workings of women's minds."

The corners of her mouth threatened a smile, but she held it in check admirably. "Gotcha. Trust me, I say what I think. If someone is too dense to get it, I spell it out in simpler language again and again until I get down to their level."

"You saying I'm dense?"

"Never."

Reaching over, he tugged her ponytail. "You are not going to play games like other women do or I'll have to take you down a peg or two."

Laughing, she buckled her seat belt. "Whatever guy tangles with me is going to know exactly where he stands."

FIRST THING THE NEXT MORNING, Vince called Mariah and she promised to have the bike ready by close of business. The freedom of the road was sounding better and better.

On the way to one of his job sites, Vince stopped at a florist, then made a side trip and pulled into the cemetery. He hadn't been there in a couple of months and for some reason today he needed the sanity.

He parked under the sprawling pecan tree and squatted down to face Matt's headstone. "Hey, kid. Just wanted to check in. Been thinking about you a lot lately. Kenzie's been bringing another kid around to play ball and stuff and he reminds me of what you and I never had a chance to do. Hope you don't mind. Nah, you wouldn't mind. You'd be a couple years older than him, but you'd get along. I miss you, Matt."

He turned to Belinda's headstone and removed the bouquet of faded silk daisies he and Kenzie had brought for her thirty-fifth birthday back in February. He laid them aside and placed the bouquet of Texas wildflowers in the vase beside the monument.

He wasn't surprised to look up and see Gray's truck bounce through the gate. It wasn't the first time they'd bumped into each other here. Something about twins. At first Vince had kept the area clean, but since Grayson had returned from the navy and started the landscaping business, the gravesite had become his pet project.

Vince ran a hand over Belinda's headstone. "Hey there, babe. Our baby girl is growing into a beautiful young lady, in spite of me. You'd be proud of her. Me, I'm not sure I'm handling things so well, but what else is new, huh?"

The old truck rattled to a stop behind Vince's pickup, and Gray walked up and knelt down beside him. "She'd be okay with this, you know. With you finally finding someone."

Vince rubbed his forehead. "I know. Belinda isn't the problem. Hanna is."

Gray got that "I knew it" look on his face, plucked a dandelion and looked around for any other weeds that might have popped out since he last visited. "Remember the first time you spent a Sunday at the house before you and Belinda worked out the whole baby thing? You hardly opened your mouth to anyone except Dad and Belinda."

"That was different."

Gray shook his head. "Yeah, you had a genuine goal in being there, but the chaos was pretty overwhelming, no?"

Vince closed his eyes. "And that was even before there were so many kids. You don't have to tell me that I sort of left Hanna hanging out to dry, but I was busy watching the kids, keeping Wayne from burning the burgers and generally doing what we do."

I didn't pay enough attention to her at the folks' house and she breaks it off? What's up with that? If that was what had

*her panties in a twist, she could have said something while
we were there instead of stewing over it.*

"Hanna wouldn't let one afternoon mess things up," Gray
said, reading his thoughts. "I talked to her, but she said she
didn't need babysitting."

There were still pieces missing. "There has to be something
else."

"Look. You seem pretty serious about Hanna. Try talking
to her."

First Mackenzie and now Gray. Was it that obvious? "Got
shut down. She broke it off. I'm not into groveling." Hanna
knew where to find him if she got over whatever bee was in
her bonnet.

Gray straightened and tossed the dead daisies and weeds
into the trash can beside the road. "Then I guess you'd just
as soon spend your evenings playing video games with
Kenzie."

Vince raised an eyebrow.

"You sure Kenzie isn't part of the problem? No jealousy?
You two are tight and she might not like Hanna encroaching
on her territory."

Vince winced. "Kenzie's not really happy. Not sure she
totally understands. I mean, how do you tell a twelve-year-old
that her old man needs a woman in his life?"

"Haven't had that sex talk yet, huh?"

"We're both sort of avoiding it. Can't you just hear that
conversation? Kenzie will be grossed out."

"You might be amazed how much she already understands.
Kids grow up fast these days."

Oh, God. "And I thought diapers stunk."

"You could ask Mom to talk to her."

"Thought about that. But Kenzie's my daughter. I'm working up to it." Vince grinned. "Want to assist?"

Gray turned ashen. "I'd love to, but I have to scrub the toilet that evening."

Pretty much the response he'd expected. "Some uncle you are."

Chapter Eighteen

Vince had two crews working, and by the end of the day every last one of them was probably ready to quit. Today he wasn't taking any crap from anyone. They either did the job the way it was designed or they were damn well going to hear about it.

Gray pulled up to the site just as Vince was tearing into the foreman about not staying on top of the guy sawing the timbers. "You just cost me two hundred bucks. If he doesn't know how to read the damn plans, put someone else on the saw."

"The kid made a mistake."

"Then the kid is back to using a nail gun and if he can't handle that, he can try his luck sacking groceries."

Gray nodded toward the truck. "Ready to pick up the Harley?"

Vince glanced at his watch. "I thought you were going to meet me at the house."

"Hey, don't snap my head off. I had a job just down the street. But if you don't need a ride, I've got a cold beer with my name on it waiting at home."

Vince gritted his teeth. "No need to get all testy." He locked his pickup, took a deep breath and crawled into Gray's. "Sorry. Been a bad day."

Gray turned the key and waited for the engine to kick in. He pumped the gas a couple times and the engine finally caught. "Lighten up. It's not their fault your love life tanked."

Vince acknowledged this remark with an obscene hand gesture that only earned him a laugh from his brother-in-law.

Vince blew off steam. "I mean, what the hell happened? One day everything was going great, then out of the blue, Hanna said it's over. What changed?"

Gray shrugged as he stopped at an intersection to let an eighteen-wheeler pass.

"Not only do women expect us to understand what they say, they also seem to think we can read their minds." Vince was getting worked up all over again just thinking about it. "How the hell are we supposed to keep up?"

Gray cocked an eyebrow and shifted into third.

"What does she expect me to do? Does she think I'll come knocking at her door? Is it a game? Or maybe she really does just want me to disappear."

"Bullshit," Gray said.

Vince wanted to think it was just a temporary bump in the road, but he wasn't sure. "There was something between us and it was more than San Antonio and sex. We connect. She tried to walk away once and came back, so why is she doing it again?"

Gray gave him a sideways smirk as they started across the bridge.

"Should I call her, you think?" Vince stared straight ahead. "No way. That's what she wants me to do."

"So you're both hardheaded? That'll turn out well."

Vince glared at him. "I thought she'd call me when she worked through things with Richard, but now I wonder. She'll call." Vince stared out the window at the field of late-blooming pink buttercups, trying to convince himself. "Won't she?"

Gray pulled into the parking lot and held up both hands.

"When did I suddenly become the expert? Look at my love life."

"What love life?"

Gray grimaced. "My point exactly."

Vince slid out of the truck and eyed Mariah's cute little figure. She was a couple of inches shorter than Hanna, not a single curl in her cropped brown hair. But the whole package fitted together nicely, right down to those tight jeans and tank top.

Gray, apparently, was oblivious.

Mariah looked up from a bike and flashed a pair of green eyes. "Bike's ready. Take it for a spin and see how it performs."

It was still too early for afternoon rush hour, not that rush hour in Marble Falls amounted to much. Heading away from town, he opened the bike up. The engine purred like a tiger. When he got back to the shop, Mariah was working on another bike and Gray was in the parking lot, leaning against the truck as if there wasn't a good-looking woman twenty feet away.

"Trust me, the woman has magic hands."

Gray shook his head. "You're the one who shares with her the thrill of risking life and limb on a two-wheeled get-ya-killed."

Giving him a go-to-hell look, Vince went to pay Mariah. He should ask her out. He'd thought about it a time or two, but then he'd met Hanna. He wrote out the check. "You do have a way with a machine, Ms. Calabrezie."

Her smile was sweet. "We all have our quirks. Personally I find that engines make more sense than most people."

"You called that one right." He handed her the check and took the receipt. "Take care."

"So, did you ask her out?" Gray asked as Vince coasted to a stop beside the truck.

Why, when he looked at Mariah, did he only see what

wasn't like Hanna Rosser? That should have been a good thing. "Just follow me home to drop off the bike."

"Figured she might be your type."

"She's a doll, but I've had about all the small-town gossip I can stomach this week. Austin is looking better and better."

Gray grinned and pulled out of the lot. They dropped off the bike and picked up Kenzie at the house, then headed back to the job site for Vince's pickup.

"Uncle Gray, you coming to my graduation next Friday?"

Kenzie had a special bond with her mother's twin and it made Vince both happy and sad. Belinda had adored Matt, but she'd doted on her baby girl.

Gray nudged Kenzie. "You sure your grades are good enough that they're actually going to let you graduate from elementary school?"

"I've got it," Kenzie said from her perch between the two men. "I could sign you up for that show *Are You Smarter Than a Fifth Grader?* and maybe you'd have to eat a few of those words."

Vince offered to buy Gray dinner, but he declined, so Vince and Kenzie headed for Wal-Mart to pick up groceries and dog food. Vince wasn't in the mood to eat out. Maybe they'd grill hamburgers.

Kenzie made her way through the aisles doing what Kenzie was best at, tossing cookies and chips into the basket. Vince turned down an aisle and almost ran his shopping cart into Hanna's. Their gazes met for a split second before she looked away.

"Hello, Ms. Rosser." Kenzie tossed in a bag of Oreos and stood in front of Vince, facing Hanna. "Where's Ash?"

"He's home, doing his homework." Those sad, dark eyes looked up from Kenzie and focused on him. "Vince."

"Hanna."

His gut hurt. His body had an elemental reaction to hers. He wanted to drag her aside and make her admit that what they had was worth fighting for.

Instead, he stood motionless and watched her walk away. She'd ended it. She could make the first move to get it back. If she wanted it back.

HANNA HELD HER HEAD HIGH and forced one foot in front of the other. If she didn't look into those denim-colored eyes, maybe she could resist the spell Vince had over her. Maybe she could not lie awake again tonight and wonder if she'd lost her ever-loving mind for ending it with him.

But they had rushed into a physical relationship too soon. Before she'd had time to get her head together after the divorce.

The night before, when her thoughts had been in so much turmoil over Vince that she couldn't sleep, she'd tried to picture her life back in Dallas. As much as she'd loved her beautiful home, it was no longer what she wanted. There was more to it than her unwillingness to forgive Richard; her dreams had changed. She might not know yet what the future held, but she knew she had to make it happen on her own.

Vince hadn't called or stopped by, but that was what she'd needed, right? Time to regroup, to get to know who Hanna was after the divorce.

Who was she kidding? Time wasn't an issue. Vince had her so wrapped around his finger, she couldn't stop thinking about him. She just wasn't willing to play second fiddle to Belinda for the rest of her life. Or to the entire Maguire clan.

She tossed a bundle of leaf lettuce in the basket with the six-pack of underwear for Ashton and went in search of French bread for dinner. It really was amazing how much money she saved by shopping at Wal-Mart. The identical underwear would be twice as much at the department store in Dallas.

At the checkout counter she picked up one of those flashy, sensationalized star rags, but glanced at the headlines and put it back. Who really believed any of that crap? It was mean-spirited gossip, just like the kind in small towns, only on a worldwide scale.

BLUEBONNET BOOKS WAS QUIET Thursday afternoon. Norma had taken off to meet her friends for lunch and their weekly bridge game. Customers were evidently staying in out of the rain, or at least they weren't into reading. Hanna was sitting behind the counter filling out an order when she heard the bell on the door jingle.

Vince looked incredibly serious, dressed in jeans and the same black button-down he'd worn in San Antonio. He closed the door against the dark clouds and brushed the rain off his arms.

As he turned, their eyes met, but he stayed in the front of the store. Placing both palms on the windowsill, he leaned his weight on them and crossed one ankle over the other. Those intense eyes bored a hole into her soul.

"Hi," she said. Anything to break the silence.

"Hi." He looked up, then back at her as if he wasn't sure what to say. "I talked to Claire this morning."

Hanna's breath caught in her throat. "About?"

"You. Us. The past. The future."

She wasn't sure what that meant. "To ask her permission?"

He shook his head. "First, I need you to tell me why you broke it off after the barbecue. No games, Hanna."

She closed her eyes. She couldn't do this. Slowly she opened her eyes and looked at him. Okay, he wanted honesty. "I know Belinda was a wonderful person. And I know that you all loved her very much. You will always be a part of the Maguire family. I'm just not sure there's any room left for me."

"Fair enough." He continued to lean on the windowsill. "Belinda's family has been very good to me. I owed it to Claire at least to hear it from me. No matter how much I loved Belinda, it's time to move past that."

She stared at him in disbelief. "Vince."

"Hear me out before you say anything." He cocked one eyebrow. "I took your advice. I've registered for a summer class to finish my master's. And I talked to my old boss about some opportunities here and maybe eventually abroad."

"Oh." Hanna nibbled at her lip. So this wasn't about getting back together? It was about him moving on? She'd waited too long to tell him she loved him. She blinked at the realization. She. Loved. Him. Fighting back tears, she mustered up fake enthusiasm. "I'm so proud of you for following your dream. Living abroad will be an amazing experience for Mackenzie."

He pushed off the windowsill and took a step forward.

Don't touch me. I can't handle that. If you don't touch me, maybe I won't break down completely until I get home. Maybe I won't beg for another chance.

He took a second step and wrapped a curl of her hair around his finger. "Dreams change. I thought I could just move on and put us behind me." He slid a hand behind her neck and drew her closer. "I never thought I'd be in love again. This all-out, don't-want-to-waste-a-day-without-you sort of love." He ran the back of his hand down her cheek. "Living abroad could be an awesome experience for Ashton, too. And us."

Her heart raced and she couldn't tear her eyes away.

Tilting his head, he smiled. "I love you. I want you with me."

She stared at his gorgeous, sexy mouth as it descended toward hers. She parted her lips and reacquainted herself with the taste and feel of Vince. Wrapping her arms around him, she pulled him as close as she could, craving his touch. She rested her palm against his face and studied every single inch of him.

"It'll take at least a couple of years to finish school and get some experience under my belt. Give you time to…"

"Shh." She put her finger to his lips, still moist from the kiss. She ran a hand down his clean-shaven cheek, enjoying the sheer masculine realness of it. "I don't need time. As hard as I've tried not to, I've thought about nothing but you since you walked out of here the other day. I love you, Vince Keegan."

She leaned back against the wall, watching him, waiting.

He groaned and placed his hands on either side of her head and leaned in, pressing all six feet, two inches of his body against hers. She ran her hands down his abs, around his waist and cupped his tight buttocks. Couldn't get enough of the feel of his hardness pressing into her softness. The taste of his mouth, his skin.

Pulling back just enough so she could draw a breath, she touched his face and stared into those blue eyes. "We can make an amazing life for us and the kids. Whether it's here, Austin or overseas."

He ran the back of his hand intimately down the side of her breast. "What about Bluebonnet Books?"

Tingles ran up her spine. "I love the bookstore, but Mom is ten times better than I am at knowing what people want and selling it to them. She's not good at the accounts, though. If the time comes, she and I can work something out."

"You're serious about this? I don't do well with male-female games."

She tightened her arms around him and nuzzled into his neck. "Oh, man. You're the one who better be serious, because I have no intentions of letting you go again."

Hanna's cell phone chimed and she fished it out of her pocket. "Hello."

"I'm sorry to disturb you, Ms. Rosser, but Ashton has been in a fight. We need you to come to the school."

Her heart stopped. "I'll be right there."

She hung up just as Vince's cell rang.

Hanna locked the store and put up the closed sign, then jumped into the truck with Vince. They covered the blocks to the school in no time, and Vince helped her out and they darted through the rain. He held the door open for her and they walked into the office together. William Baer already waited in front of the receptionist desk.

"Vince. Ms. Rosser."

Vince shook his hand. "Will."

Principal Montgomery stepped out and motioned for them to enter her office. All three kids sat in chairs in front of her desk. Kenzie's ponytail was falling down. Ashton had a black eye and Billy held a damp, bloody rag to his nose.

"Okay, students. One more time. Who threw the first punch?" the principal asked.

They all exchanged glances.

"I did." Ashton stood up. "He said that Kenzie's dad was having sex with my mom and that she was a ho."

"Well, they are," Billy said. "You're not supposed to hit a guy for telling the truth."

Kenzie jumped to her feet. "What my dad does is none of your business. And Ms. Rosser is not a ho. You say that again and I'll pound you into dog poop."

Hanna's mouth dropped open. Kenzie defending her?

William Baer glanced from Hanna to Vince, then focused on his son. "Billy, you know better than to say things like that."

Hanna tried to stay calm. The way Mr. Baer had looked her up and down, he obviously believed the rumors. Probably where Billy had heard them to begin with.

Principal Montgomery stared at Ashton. "This school does

not condone fighting. You were in the wrong for striking another child. Do you understand that if I suspend you, you won't be allowed to graduate with your class tomorrow?"

Vince stepped forward. "Excuse me, Mrs. Montgomery. But you can't really hold it against a boy for defending his mother. I would have thought that behavior would be rewarded, not punished."

Hanna felt a sick ache in her stomach. A straight-A kid and he was in danger of not graduating because of her.

William Baer clamped a hand on his son's shoulder. "Billy. I expect you to apologize to Ashton and to the other people in this room. Your remark was inappropriate."

Ashton held his head high and stared at Billy, waiting. Kenzie stood beside him, united with him.

"I'm sorry." Billy shuffled his feet. "I shouldn't have said it."

He started to sit back down, but his father turned him toward Vince and Hanna.

Obviously uncomfortable, Billy laid the bloody rag on the chair and stuffed his hands into his pockets. "I'm sorry. I didn't really mean it. It's just that Ash gets so riled up these days. I couldn't help myself."

"Apology accepted." Hanna turned to Ashton. "You should forgive Billy."

"Okay." Ashton took a step forward and shook Billy's hand. "Just no more remarks about my mom or Vince."

Principal Montgomery took a deep breath. "Well, we only have a half day tomorrow, then graduation. Surely we can let this one pass and get through tomorrow without further incident."

Hanna shook the woman's hand. "Thank you, Mrs. Montgomery. I appreciate your decision."

Hanna and Ashton walked out of the school with Vince

and Kenzie. She wasn't sure what to say to the kids about the recent turn of events.

The rain had moved out, but water ran down the curbs along the parking lot and dripped from the overhanging trees.

Ashton looked around. "Where's the car?"

"I rode with Vince." She watched Ashton's face for a reaction. Would he put two and two together? He'd known they were no longer seeing each other.

"Does this mean we're going to be a family?" Mackenzie blurted out.

Vince exchanged looks with Hanna, waiting for her to answer.

"There is that possibility." She watched the kids closely. "How do you two feel about that? Kenzie?"

Kenzie widened her eyes at Ashton, then they both erupted into giggles.

"Cool," Kenzie said.

Ashton high-fived Kenzie. "They don't know how much trouble they're in."

* * * * *

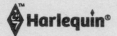

Harlequin®

American ★ Romance®

COMING NEXT MONTH

Available April 12, 2011

#1349 MY FAVORITE COWBOY
American Romance's Men of the West
Shelley Galloway

#1350 ONE WILD COWBOY
Texas Legacies: The McCabes
Cathy Gillen Thacker

#1351 A CONVENIENT PROPOSAL
Creature Comforts
Lynnette Kent

#1352 RODEO DADDY
Rodeo Rebels
Marin Thomas

REQUEST YOUR FREE BOOKS!
2 FREE NOVELS PLUS 2 FREE GIFTS!

🔷 **Harlequin**®

American ★ *Romance*®

LOVE, HOME & HAPPINESS

YES! Please send me 2 FREE Harlequin American Romance® novels and my 2 FREE gifts (gifts are worth about $10). After receiving them, if I don't wish to receive any more books, I can return the shipping statement marked "cancel." If I don't cancel, I will receive 4 brand-new novels every month and be billed just $4.24 per book in the U.S. or $4.99 per book in Canada. That's a saving of at least 15% off the cover price! It's quite a bargain! Shipping and handling is just 50¢ per book in the U.S. and 75¢ per book in Canada.* I understand that accepting the 2 free books and gifts places me under no obligation to buy anything. I can always return a shipment and cancel at any time. Even if I never buy another book, the two free books and gifts are mine to keep forever.

154/354 HDN FDKS

Name	(PLEASE PRINT)

Address	Apt. #

City	State/Prov.	Zip/Postal Code

Signature (if under 18, a parent or guardian must sign)

Mail to the **Reader Service:**
IN U.S.A.: P.O. Box 1867, Buffalo, NY 14240-1867
IN CANADA: P.O. Box 609, Fort Erie, Ontario L2A 5X3

Not valid for current subscribers to Harlequin American Romance books.

Want to try two free books from another line?
Call 1-800-873-8635 or visit www.ReaderService.com.

* Terms and prices subject to change without notice. Prices do not include applicable taxes. Sales tax applicable in N.Y. Canadian residents will be charged applicable taxes. Offer not valid in Quebec. This offer is limited to one order per household. All orders subject to credit approval. Credit or debit balances in a customer's account(s) may be offset by any other outstanding balance owed by or to the customer. Please allow 4 to 6 weeks for delivery. Offer available while quantities last.

Your Privacy—The Reader Service is committed to protecting your privacy. Our Privacy Policy is available online at www.ReaderService.com or upon request from the Reader Service.

We make a portion of our mailing list available to reputable third parties that offer products we believe may interest you. If you prefer that we not exchange your name with third parties, or if you wish to clarify or modify your communication preferences, please visit us at www.ReaderService.com/consumerschoice or write to us at Reader Service Preference Service, P.O. Box 9062, Buffalo, NY 14269. Include your complete name and address.

HAR11

Selene wanted nothing to do with the father of her son, Alex; but Aristedes had other plans…that included them.

Read on for an sneak peek from
THE SARANTOS SECRET BABY by Olivia Gates,
available April 2011, only from Harlequin Desire.

"You were right to turn my marriage offer down," Aristedes said.

And Selene found her voice at last, found the words that would not betray the blow he'd dealt her. "Thanks for letting me know. You didn't have to come all the way here, though. You could have just let it go. I left yesterday with the understanding that this case is closed."

Before the hot needles behind her eyes could dissolve into an unforgivable display of stupidity and weakness, she began to close the door.

The door stopped against an immovable object. His flat palm.

"I can't accept that." His voice was low, leashed.

What did her tormentor mean now? Was he ending one game only to start another?

She raised eyes as bruised as her self-respect to his, found nothing there but solemnity and determination.

Before she could voice her confusion, he elaborated. "I never let anything go unless I'm certain it's unworkable. I realize I made you an unworkable offer, and that's why I'm withdrawing it. I'm here to offer something else. A workability study."

She leaned against the door, thankful for its support and partial shield. "Your son and I are not a business venture you can test for feasibility."

His gaze grew deeper, made her feel as if he was trying to delve into her mind, take control of it. "It's actually the other way around. I'm the one who would be tested."

She shook her head. "Why bother? I know—and *you* know—you're not workable. Not with me."

His spectacular eyebrows lowered over eyes she felt were emitting silver hypnosis. "You're right again. Neither you nor I have any reason to believe that isn't the truth. The only truth. It might be best for both you and Alex to never hear from me again, to forget I exist. But then again, maybe not. I'm only asking for the chance for both of us to find out for certain. You believe I'm unworkable in any personal relationship. I've lived my life based on that belief about myself. I never really had reason to question it. But I have one now. In fact, I have two."

Find out what happens in
THE SARANTOS SECRET BABY by Olivia Gates,
available April 2011, only from Harlequin Desire.